Mary Christine Zimmer

AF198159

One Week

That Is All What It Takes

JustFiction Edition

Impressum/Imprint (nur für Deutschland/only for Germany)
Bibliografische Information der Deutschen Nationalbibliothek: Die Deutsche
Nationalbibliothek verzeichnet diese Publikation in der Deutschen Nationalbibliografie;
detaillierte bibliografische Daten sind im Internet über http://dnb.d-nb.de abrufbar.
Alle in diesem Buch genannten Marken und Produktnamen unterliegen warenzeichen-,
marken- oder patentrechtlichem Schutz bzw. sind Warenzeichen oder eingetragene
Warenzeichen der jeweiligen Inhaber. Die Wiedergabe von Marken, Produktnamen,
Gebrauchsnamen, Handelsnamen, Warenbezeichnungen u.s.w. in diesem Werk berechtigt
auch ohne besondere Kennzeichnung nicht zu der Annahme, dass solche Namen im Sinne
der Warenzeichen- und Markenschutzgesetzgebung als frei zu betrachten wären und
daher von jedermann benutzt werden dürften.

Coverbild: www.ingimage.com

Verlag: JustFiction! Edition ist ein Imprint der
LAP LAMBERT Academic Publishing GmbH & Co. KG
Heinrich-Böcking-Str. 6-8, 66121 Saarbrücken, Deutschland
Telefon +49 681 37 20 310, Telefax +49 681 37 20 310-9
Email: info@justfiction-edition.com

Herstellung in Deutschland:
Schaltungsdienst Lange o.H.G., Berlin
Books on Demand GmbH, Norderstedt
Reha GmbH, Saarbrücken
Amazon Distribution GmbH, Leipzig
ISBN: 978-3-8454-4562-5

Imprint (only for USA, GB)
Bibliographic information published by the Deutsche Nationalbibliothek: The Deutsche
Nationalbibliothek lists this publication in the Deutsche Nationalbibliografie; detailed
bibliographic data are available in the Internet at http://dnb.d-nb.de.
Any brand names and product names mentioned in this book are subject to trademark,
brand or patent protection and are trademarks or registered trademarks of their respective
holders. The use of brand names, product names, common names, trade names, product
descriptions etc. even without a particular marking in this works is in no way to be
construed to mean that such names may be regarded as unrestricted in respect of
trademark and brand protection legislation and could thus be used by anyone.

Cover image: www.ingimage.com

Publisher: JustFiction! Edition
is an imprint of the publishing house
LAP LAMBERT Academic Publishing GmbH & Co. KG
Heinrich-Böcking-Str. 6-8, 66121 Saarbrücken, Germany
Phone +49 681 37 20 310, Fax +49 681 37 20 310-9
Email: info@justfiction-edition.com

Printed in the U.S.A.
Printed in the U.K. by (see last page)
ISBN: 978-3-8454-4562-5

Mary Christine Zimmer

One Week

Table of Contents

Here comes Mark Rivera again. Again for the nth time this season; I don't get why he always pick on me when there's so many other people here in the campus; considering the fact that there are approximately fifty thousand students studying here. I'm not exaggerating all this but I've experience going in and out of this campus without seeing anyone for the second time, well except for a certain Mark Rivera. I can't blame anyone to go with the flow with what he's doing even though he hurts them either physically or emotionally sometimes. Why you may ask? Well simply because he is our school's pride, he's none other than our basketball superstar, such a stuck-up jerk.

There she is again, Cassey Garcia, with the books piled up again covering her face. I can't understand why she loves books so much, considering that it's boring and heavy at the same time and all the other reasons to hate it more. Besides however hard you study, there's always an open possibility to failure and close possibility to passing. No, not really, I just exaggerated that part, but depending on what failure is, it might be true. If you're one of the nerds, not getting an 'A' is nothing but a failure, and for us jocks, getting a 'C' is passing, and below it is failure, which is true given the grading system of this school. Well enough with the grades, but really if you ask me this campus would be much nicer in her sight if only she could see it, like exactly right now.

WHAM! No not again! This is the third time this week. I just have to step on that banana peel again. I should have learned that by now, but no! I slipped AGAIN! Probably he's doing again, look at him grin, Aargh how I hate him so much!

This is why I love teasing her so much, she is so affected, and well in other words, she always gets it. I always get a good laugh, a nice way to start the day. Oops that's the bell, got to get out of her sight or I'll be late again like yesterday.

Aargh! He took off! If I could get my hands on him, he is so dead! Back to picking up these books again, before I be late AGAIN! Oh, how I hate mornings like this, but on the other hand this is just the start there's still afternoon and evening to enjoy this.

-12:00-

Finally! Lunch time, I am so famished. I am not able to eat breakfast since there's none at home. Thank God its lunch time, I am so thankful.

Finally! Lunch time, I'm so hungry. The lesson's so mind challenging, it's making me hungry. I wonder how everyone else is doing. Are they the same as me? What about her? She seems to be enjoying herself.

Oh no the line!

Aargh! Finally! My turn

"Excuse me, but I got in the line first" A deep voice protests.

"Excuse me, but I was here first." She protests back.

"Look Cassey, I'm trying not to be rude here, but could you please let me have my meal then go after me." He suggests.

"No! I stood here first, besides lady's first." She said smiling at her soon victory.

"Fine! Have it your way" he growls.

"Oh I'm sorry, you want to go first? Oops sorry never noticed that you're a lady, I always thought you're a man." Teasing him

"No, thank you, lady's first" he said twitching an eyebrow.

People on the background started to giggle.

Ha! Finally I got back at him, *giggles*

4

She's so going to pay for this, just watch and see Cassey! I'll have my day

-15:30-

Finally the bell, I am so out of here. Got to go to the gym for an early practice to warm up, superstar way.

Oh that's the bell; I got to fix my things quick. I can't be late for my library duty. How unfortunate for me to be stuck at the library every Wednesday afternoon, to pick up those jerks trash. Not trash, literally, but the books they scattered around the table, not even making an effort to return them properly on the shelf, but some do return those books but to different shelves; and their worst trash are those books they throw to the floor, not bothering to pick it up and return then or even put it on the table. Sometimes I like walking up to them and say what's your problem, books are essentials you know. But no, couldn't do it, I could get in trouble.

Lucky! There's still no one here in the gym, I could get a good warm up; finally some peace in playing my one and only love, basketball. No coach to yell at me, no team mates to bug me, and no school to pressure me, it's just me and my sport. And maybe I could use this time to think how I can get back at her for doing that to me during Lunch time. I need to get back at her; I wouldn't accept defeat, especially not from her.

-19:00-

Finally, my duty's over, I could finally rest. I think I'd stay here for a while, to relax a bit for a change, the school park looks like a nice place, since no one would be around at this time of hour, I think. I just have to lock the library and I'm on my way to paradise.

End of practice finally! I can't wait to relax at my favorite spot, the school park. I could see the stars shinning brightly at the vast horizon in front of my very eyes. Finally I could have a time for myself; a time of peace in my heart. No pressure. No stress. No worries. No noise.

Peace! How I love peace, it's so nice here, I wonder why I never come here, and this is so relaxing. I think I'd come back here more often.

What is that girl doing here?! That's my spot, how could she?! Aargh! That girl's going to get it.

"Get out of my bench!" He ordered.

"Excuse me?" She asks innocently while looking up, and surprised to see who it was, and how he looks at her angrily.

"What are you doing here?" She asks nervously.

"That's my bench you're sitting." He exclaimed.

"I don't believe seeing your name anywhere on this bench" She said as a matter of fact.

"I don't care! Just get out of my bench!" He ordered her raising his voice.

"Don't you dare raise your voice on me" She stood up facing him face to face.

Why this jerk! He thinks I'm just going to let it pass like everything he's been doing to me.

This punk is getting on my nerves! Aargh! My night is so ruined because of this stupid nerd right in front of me. Can't she just get it?

I can't stand him/her.

"Let's just share this bench to end all of this nonsense." She suggests

"No!" He exclaimed, directing his point.

"Why can't you just share this bench, it's not like you own it." She said as calm as possible.

"You don't know anything okay?! Just leave before I'm completely tick off." He said not really in the mood to argue anymore.

"So what; I really don't care about you, and you can't make me leave, if this is uncomfortable with you then just leave, no one's going to stop you, you know." She explained.

"You! Why you brat! I can't stand you anymore; you think you're funny huh? You just don't know what I've been through this night, you know what? Let's make a bet." He suggests.

"What kind" She asks curiously.

"Let's switch lives for a week, what do you say?" He said grinning.

"You don't know what you're talking about; you can't handle my life you know." She said honestly.

"Yeah right! Maybe you're just scared because you can't do it. Chicken!" He teases, grinning widely.

"Okay! If you really want to, but don't blame me if you can't make it, don't say I didn't warn you." She said calmly and honestly.

"Let's start next Monday, that'll give us enough time to fix things, like what to say with our parents and the faculty." He said.

"Oh and don't forget to make a schedule, I don't want to mix your activities"

"Okay, you too" He agreed.

"That wouldn't be a problem." She grinned.

I can't believe he's so into this. He's so going to suffer, he just don't have the slightest idea what he got himself to.

She's so dumb, can't believe she's a nerd. Does she honestly think she can handle my life? Basketball is already too much for her. She's so going to suffer that week.

And they laughed inside.

-Sunday-

Three days have passed since that 'talk', tomorrow's the big day. Got to go get my bag ready before he arrives; for him to stay and me to walk out. I almost forgot my private stuffs, I should hide it, but we made a promise, what am I going to do?

Ding! Dong! This is it. I wonder how their house looks like; I sure hope it's breathable. Is she ready? I hope so, I am very enthusiastic about this idea, and she's not going to ruin it for me don't she dare back out this last minute. Here she comes, finally. *Sigh*

"You know that it's just for a week, right?" He said pointing out his point.

"Yes, my bag is just big not much inside, don't worry." She assured him.

"Well, tomorrow's the day, oh and before I forget don't you dare trash my room." He warned her.

"Same to you, and don't forget to follow your schedule okay?" She confirms.

"Of course same to you, bye!" He exhaled deep while closing the door.

He still hasn't got the slightest idea on what he got himself too. I wonder what's his plans, how is he going to survive this week? *Giggles* he's going to lose this bet big time.

She thinks she could really do this, how pathetic. She's going to regret this, she don't have the slightest idea what she got herself into in the first place. She's going to give up sooner or later, I just know it, and I'll win this for sure.

~Chapter 1: Monday~

Yawn It's a good thing he has flat pillow, or sleeping would be a problem, and I don't want that to happen. I wonder what's in store for me today.

Yawn It's a good thing she uses flat pillow, feels just like at home. Now lets me see what's in it for me today. Let me see her or rather my schedule.

Stared wide-eyed "I can't believed this"

He got so much time, no wonder he's such a jerk. Mental note: Basketball practice at four.

Is she human? Her schedule is all piled up. No I don't think this is real but… It looks like it's not new, like it has been there since the start of school. Mental note: Cafeteria Duty after lunch.

I'll make this day, I'll show him/her.

There he is right now! Aargh! This man is so lazy, where's all the books? You are so in trouble mister!

Look like she's on her way towards me, bet she thought I'm lazy. Ha! In her face! I'm popular; many would want to carry all those books for me.

Aargh that jerk! Using his popularity, he's so going to suffer this, especially after the announcement. I'm so going to enjoy this, seeing him die in embarrassment. *Laughs*

Announcement Students! Seems like two of our students are facing difficult challenge at the moment; they have switched lives for a week, so please bear with them. Starting from today Mr. Mark Rivera is Ms. Cassey Garcia and vice versa. I have already talked with the faculty; their only plea is that you cooperate with them. Thank you.

Too early for that announcement, ouch! That hurts, these guys can really throw books, and they are so rude. They didn't have to follow what the principal said immediately.

Laughs Let the day begin. You're so lucky I won't be making fun of you this time, seeing those books thrown at you is already enough for today's good laugh.

-12:00-

Finally lunch time, I am so famished. I can't believe they don't have anything prepared for breakfast. I think I'm going to die sooner or later if this continues.

What? Over already? I was expecting more time; I didn't get hungry, maybe because I ate toast with jam served with a glass of milk this morning, which I don't really take. Life is sweet; I think I'm going to enjoy this swap.

Here she is again in front of me; I am so famished even to pick a fight.

"Hey! You could go first." She insisted, giving him way.

"T-Thanks" surprised.

Wonder what got into her. She's not arguing with me, she just let me go first. It's so unusual, but who cares as long as I got my meal. I'm in heaven. I haven't eaten like this before, not paying much attention to what the food looks like or what it smells like or even taste like, I just eat and eat and eat.

He's so regretting it, me being nice to him all of a sudden, despite of everything that had happened. He's just lucky that's my life he's living right now, and I know how famished he is at the moment. Lucky for him I am nice. Though eating breakfast would be so much fun, having tons of energy for the classes, but it's lonely though no one to eat with you they just serve you your meal and that's all the company you get.

One last bite, yum! I am so full; I wonder how she manages this, not eating breakfast. Breakfast is such an essential meal of the day, my mom used to say or so I thought, that's what they told me. That is why they always make sure that I eat my breakfast everyday before going to school, no matter how late I would be. Now I understand why she's so persistent in getting in the line first, before I thought it's because she didn't want left-over to be served at her, but now things changed.

Wonder what he's thinking, he looks serious just a moment ago when he finished his meal. I wonder if he now understands why I always rush in the cafeteria. The big challenge is now, how could he last it. How did he even manage it for today?

-13:30-

Cafeteria Duty. Wow! I can't believe I'm doing this, washing all this, not just that I also got to sweep and mop the floor. I am beginning to think she's doing this on purpose, making a joke out of my innocence. She's going to pay big time if I find out.

"This is so tiring" he complains.

"Cassey never complained." A lady with sweet voice clarifies.

"That's because she's used to it" he protests.

"No, ever since she started never did once she complained about this." She answered honestly.

"Yeah whatever! Look lady if you're just here to insult me might as well just leave me in peace to do my work." He said rather irritated.

"Cassey usually does this all by herself, but she begged me to give you a hand. What would a friend to do?" she answered as a matter of fact.

"And why would she do that?" he asks curiously.

"Well she told me she just couldn't bear having a bad record in her duty, so here I am to help."

"If you think I can't do it, then watch this and tell that friend of yours."

11

"Just do your job, and pretend I'm not here okay?"

Cassey was right, he is a jerk. I can't believe I admire him. I am so pissed off by his arrogance. I'll just finish this and get done with, can't disappoint Cassey.

I wonder what's going on with her mind, first the lunch line and now this, a helping hand for her duty. What exactly are you thinking Cassey Garcia?

-15:45-

It has been a long time since I've step in this court and even a longer time since I've hold this ball. It feels like the same as before; like nothing has changed. I think I can't do this, not anymore since that incident. I wonder what they would let me do. Do they plan on letting me join their practice or just let me do something else? I do hope they'll just let me do something else, like acting manager and stuff. But what if I'm forced to play, but then I couldn't possibly play like them, so probably they wouldn't let me in it. They wouldn't take the chance, it's too risky. What am I going to do? Cassey stop thinking about it, nothing bad is going to happen, just hope for the best.

-16:00-

Time for practice, this is it! God help me please.

"Everyone fall in line." The coach shouted.

When everyone is on the line, the coach said "As everyone of you know Mr. Rivera is not here with us, so I would like you to give it a hundred and ten percent every practice so you could give a hundred and twenty percent at the game.

Everyone whined when suddenly…

"Yes sir!" Cassey respond.

The coach eyed her and smiles to himself and pointed her "You, jog all throughout practice session, you would only stop if I say so, clear?"

"Crystal clear sir." She answered

She gets on her position and jog slowly.

Everyone begin to eye her and murmurs grow.

"What are you still standing there? Let's go! Go! Go!"

She's quite disciplined, considering what Mark told me 'she's a nerd coach, she can't possibly play, just let her jog or something.' But more than anyone here, even Mark, she's an exception. She followed orders without anything to say, not even whining like this guys or showing me her pity look. She's a lady but look at how she run, she's good, and she got good pacing. She's magnificent, wonder how long she'll last it.

I didn't expect that, letting me run the whole practice time. This has got to stop sooner or later, I'm afraid that my old injury would take its toll. I will be in big trouble if that happens. I got to keep this pace. I got to no matter what! I've got no choice, I can't let them know I have past injuries, they'll know who I am.

-17:30-

I think she's not going to make it, she got to stop now.

"You! Mr. Rivera's substitute, you can stop now."

Finally I got to stop this; I should slow down my pace so it wouldn't be a problem.

"Hey you! Nerd, the coach said you could stop now" one of the player said.

"How nice of you to offer, continue her last one and a half hours of jogging."

13

"But coach--"

"What's that? Did I hear a whine? Drop and give me fifty, then continue the jog where she left of."

Impressive! Knowing how to stop properly, she's got talent. I wonder why she didn't join the women's team. She'll be of great help, with that height of hers, it could be an advantage.

Finally, I could stop. It's over. Hope they'll let me go now, I don't think I could still make it.

She can breathe properly too, hmm... Impressive, unlike these boys after running so much they hyperventilate for some time before breathing properly. I'll let her rest for a while and see if she can play ball. I think I'm going to enjoy watching this.

-19:00-

My body's soar all over, that coach truly is something. I got no training and he made me suffer that. I'm beat and I'm hungry, I think I'm going to die, need to sit down. Though it's stressing, it's really a fun thing to start this week. I think I can manage this. I hope so.

Finally, I've been waiting for her for ages. I wonder what coach let her do; she should have been out an hour ago. The meal's cold now, would she still take it? What if she didn't? What am I thinking? Of course, she'll take this, she'd be hungry by now, and she got no other choice but to take it.

I am so tired to argue with him, why is he here anyways? He should've been home hours ago. This man just doesn't know when to stop. I'm just starting to appreciate this day and this is all what I get, to see his face again? Aargh! But, what's that on his hands? Could it be?

"Here" Handing her the paper bag

"What's this?" She asks out of curiosity.

"Something to eat, I know you must be hungry." He shyly said.

14

"Thanks! I'm starved; I thought I'm going to die from hunger. Thank you so very much."
Taking the bag

"T-Thanks about earlier" He said rather embarrassed.

"Pardon me?" She apologized.

"About earlier, the help and all" Blushing furiously.

"Ah! That? Don't mention it, thanks for the food again, I got to go, bye." She sincerely said.

I can't believe he's being nice. What got into him? All I did was let him go first and give him a helping hand on my job, nothing to thank for. Oh no! He must have taken it differently at what I wanted to say... Well never mind, I'll just let it be for a while. There's not much to do anymore anyways.

-20:20-

"I'm Home!" Shouting to the hallowed corners of this house

Is this what welcomes him every day? A quiet house, no one around to welcome him or asks him how his day was? Nah! It couldn't be. His parents are just shy because I'm not their son that must be it.

The doors open? They didn't even bother locking their door what's with them? What if someone tried to break in or something? I might as well just lock the door, before anything happens.

"Here in this house, we have a custom of saying 'I'm home' when someone comes home." A lad older than him said.

"We also have the custom to call when we are going to be late." An old woman said.

"Oh sorry, I'm home, sorry about being late something just came up, next time I'll call, it won't happen again I'm sorry." He apologized

"Tomorrow would be your duty, since I've done yours today since you're late." The older lad speaks up again.

"Duty? What duty?" He looks worried.

"I can't believe my sister didn't tell you. Here, we take turns with the kitchen work, cooking and washing the dishes. He said.

"Sorry, I promise to do my best next time, starting tomorrow." He apologizes.

Oh no! I don't know how to cook, I never cooked anything before. Home Economics sure is useful outside school; and now I'm regretting for always skipping class and not paying much attention to it. What am I going to do? I can't simply go ask her to help me with this, could I?

Dinner's served with desserts, wow! I am enjoying this; never had desserts back at home. Lucky! Wonder how he's doing, wait! Can he even cook?

-21:00-

No more schedule. Got nothing else to do; his life is so boring. I'll just read his err--rather my notes before sleeping.

Oh no! I'm late for the schedule; I should have been studying by now. Whoa! I think I can't do this; it's just not my style, reading all this stuff.

-22:30-

Finally, time's up! I'm really sleepy… Studying could be so time consuming, hope this week will pass by quickly. What am I going to do about tomorrow's dinner? I don't even know how to cook. I'm so hopeless.

~Chapter 2: Tuesday~

Yawn I didn't get much sleep, I'm still thinking about my home duty later this night. I couldn't possibly tell them that I don't know how to cook; it'll be too much of an embarrassment. What should I do? Lord please help me... I could really use some help.

Yawn finally my body's back to normal, no pain anymore, thank God. Today's laboratory duty, wonder if he know stuffs, I usually see him dozing off during lecture.

Aargh! Stop! I don't want to think anymore. I'll ask for help, I'll swallow my pride; I can't lose my face to her family. I just couldn't let this small challenge ruin me.

Wow! Toast again, yum! I'm enjoying myself already. Yum... I wonder where his parents are, they should be used to my presence by now, and adjustment's done yesterday. Maybe later this evening they'll finally talk to me. Yeah, that's right later, I'm sure of it.

-8:00-

Here she comes, wait! She's jolly? What got into her? Though she looks pretty that way; finally revealing her face for the first time.

What is he looking at? And why is he coming this way? Please don't let him destroy my day please? It's the first time I'm enjoying myself like this, don't let him ruin this for me.

"Hey!" He greets her

"Hey!" She greets back. "What do you want?"

"I got this favor to ask... Oh never mind, just forget what I am about to say" He shyly backs away.

"Are you sure? It seems like you could use some help." She asks kindly.

17

"Yeah, thanks though" He smiled.

Wonder what his problem, maybe it's about laboratory stuffs. Don't know; don't care. He's a big boy now he can handle himself I don't need to worry about him anymore.

-12:30-

I'm famished, but my break time is not until one, wonder if there are still left-over left for me.

"Hey!" The lady yesterday greets

"Hey! What are you doing here?" He asks curiously

"Well, to bring you lunch of course" She look puzzled.

"And why would you do that?" Somewhat irritated.

"Because mister, I always bring lunch for Cassey during Tuesday, and since you're Cassey at the moment then it's your lunch. Besides she begged me to do it still so here I am." As a matter of fact

"Oh, thank you then." He said shyly

"You could eat it now if you want to; I'd do this remaining stuff over here." She suggests.

"Thanks, but I'll eat this later, by the way we haven't introduced ourselves formally, I'm Mark Rivera" Reaching out his hands

"Jacklyn Cruz" Accepting his hand

She's so lucky to have a friend that watches over her. It's a good thing she's not starving herself to death every Tuesday. Thank God.

18

"Are you normally this quiet?" She asks out of curiosity.

"Oh sorry, it's just that I don't know what to talk about." He apologizes

"We could talk about Cassey if you want to" She suggests giggling.

"W-Why would I want to talk about her?" Blushing slightly

"Yeah right, anyways just return that to her later, I'll be going now." Waving goodbye

What is she thinking? By the way she giggles; it tells me she misunderstood me. What's to talk about her? Besides Cassey must really think I'm weird after what happened yesterday and about that earlier this day.

I wonder what he's doing; did Lyn give him the meal? I hope so; he's in trouble if she didn't. Usually after lunch time, there's no more food left at the cafeteria. It's a good thing that I grew close with the cafeteria lady, or else it'll be too hard for me to talk with them about saving some bread and a juice for me. I might as well check up on him and give him a hand later after class.

I wonder how he/she's handling my life right now.

-13:35-

It's a good thing there's still some bread left and juice, just like what I hoped for. He must be starved by now; I wish Lyn remembered what I ask from her, but just to make sure.

Finally done, I could take my break now, this sure smell good, would it taste good too? I hope so. Time for me to dig in and find out

"Oh! Jacklyn remembered that's good." She exhaled deeply.

"Huh? Oh the lunch? She brought it to me earlier, thanks." He said while chewing his food.

19

"Well I'd be going now, here take this anyways." Handing the paper bag and the juice

"What's this for?"

"I thought she forgot so I bought you something to eat, so…" Not knowing how to finish her statement.

This is so embarrassing. He might think something because of this; Lyn is in big trouble if I find her. She keeps on telling me 'no' last night and I'll just find out she did what I asked of her. *Sigh* what more can I do? It already happened anyways.

"Thanks, I really appreciate it." Gratefully

"It was nothing, really, so I'll see you around?" She bid farewell.

"Wait! I need your help." He managed to say

"Help? My help? Are you Mark Rivera? What have you done to that jerk?" Raising an eyebrow

"Look! I don't know how to cook okay? You can laugh all you want but I really can't. And I can't afford to lose my face in front of your family, I just couldn't'" He said irritated, but then…

Oops! Did I say that out loud? She shouldn't hear that, oh no, I'm a laughing stock of the campus. Soon everyone will know that Mark Rivera can't cook, my popularity will be doomed. But then why do I worry so much? Why would I even care losing my face to her family, it's her family anyway? It's not like she's my girlfriend or anything.

What is he talking about? Can't bear to make a mistake in front of my folks? I think this jerk's loosing it. It must have, because he isn't eating properly like he used to. But then again, why do I feel so happy?

"Sorry, you shouldn't be enduring this, would you like to swap lives now?" Filled with concern

20

"No, I like it this way, beside it was my idea in the first place, so I won't back down. So are you going to teach me or not?"

"But how? I got class and basketball practice after, and you got office duty for an hour and a half." Looking at him for answers

"We finish at the same time right? I'll go pick you up at my- I mean your classroom and I'll talk to the coach" He suggests

"Okay, just don't get me in trouble" Wanting assurance from him

Why do I get the feeling, I/he just asks her/me out? The chills...

-14:00-

Would he really come? Is he really that desperate to make an impression? Wonder why it's so important. I want to know what he's thinking.

What is she thinking right now? How did she take what I had just said? Hope she didn't put colors to my black and white statement. Hope she'll really help me with the cooking.

-15:45-

Where is he? He should be here fifteen minutes ago. Five more minutes and that's it, I'm gone. I won't wait any longer for him; he's making me look stupid, that jerk! He's going to get it.

Oh no! Fifteen minutes has gone by, I had to hurry. Persuading coach really is hard work. Hope that she's still there, or else all my effort for him to say yes will all be put to waste.

-15:50-

That's it! Time's up! Who does he think he is anyway, acting all needy and pitiful? He's the one who needs my anyway, and here I am waiting for a miracle to happen, that jerk! I hate him!

Oh no! She's leaving. She can't leave!

"Wait up!"

"Cassey! Wait up!"

This is girl is either deaf or she's too angry to even talk with me. She's so punctual, can't believe this.

"Cassey! Hey! Wait up!"

Finally she stops…

"What?! You've wasted my time, and you still want me to help you? I'm not stupid you know"

"Sorry, coach was so hard to persuade, sorry…" Sweating and puffing a lot.

"You told me you'd pick me up then talk with the coach."

"What I said is I'll pick you up, I'll talk with the coach."

"Whatever, I'm going; you've wasted much of my time."

"Do you know how hard it is to persuade coach, and now you'll just leave? Wasting all my effort?"

"It's your fault don't blame it to me."

"Please I really need your help, I promise it won't happen again, I promise."

"Fine! You're lucky that I'm nice."

This jerk is really abusing my kindness; I'll get him for this somehow.

Thank God, she's not that far away, it's a good thing she still said yes, though she doesn't look alright. I'm beginning to be afraid of what would happen later.

"So, what are we going to cook?"

"It's your choice; you're the one who's cooking"

"I was planning to go to the wet market, would you help me pick out which is fresh and not?"

"You jerk! Don't you know anything?"

"I'm sorry, I don't cook you know. You should know that by now, I have someone to cook for me, I just wait for the serving and eat to my heart's content."

I feel sympathy for this guy, not knowing anything. Geez, that's the problem if you grew up in a rich family, not being able to do anything, depending on others for their living. This is too much for me to handle. I've finally understood why he's a jerk, and why he doesn't care about his study, he just play and play.

She looks like she's going to burst anytime soon. I've made her mad big time; she must really think I'm a jerk. She must've hated me so much by now; there'll never be any chance for us to be friends anymore. I'm doomed. Oh no! I have to be careful in my next statement.

-16:15-

Wow! The wet market looks good, but it stinks. I can't believe I'm finally here, I'd brag about this when I get back to my old life. This is so cool, me picking the meat or the vegetable or the fish I want to eat, or rather cook for me and her family. I can't wait to pick out this stuff, but I need to contain my excitement or anyone here will know I'm a newbie.

He looks like a kid who finally got the lollipop he's whining about. He looks cute, seeing him like that for the first time; excited over something so childish. He must be thinking about what to pick or what to cook later, he's so transparent. It's fun to laugh at him in this situation, being the newbie and all.

Why does she look at me like that? It's giving me the chills. Though she look happy, it's the second time I saw her smile today, actually for the entire school years that I've known her. She looks pretty that way, I hope to see that smile more often, and it fits perfectly to her face.

Why is he looking me now? He's all excited about all this earlier and now he look at me like that. He seems to blush a little; he must've noticed me making fun about his act right at this point. Oh never mind him, he's such a kid.

"Hey! You ready to pick what you would like to cook?"

"I was thinking about that vegetable over there, and this fish over here, what do you say?"

"Fine choice, let's begin then."

I can't believe I'd be enjoying this much in buying raw food at the wet market. Hope that I'll be given another chance like this, going to the wet market seeing all this vegetables, meats and fish, and having to spent time with her. Wait hold up! Where did that thought come from? Spend time with her again? I don't think so.

There he is again looking all childish in his day-dreaming mode. What is wrong with him is the smell finally reaching his brain? I hope not, I don't want to be in any trouble of sort especially that involves him.

Oh no! She notices my stare, got to look at something else. This is embarrassing. Wait! What's embarrassing about this, I'm not staring at her, I just got distracted. I have to divert her attention. I'm humiliating myself now more than ever. This is useless.

"Hey! You want to eat somewhere, when we finish here?" Hoping she'd say yes.

"Aren't we suppose to bring this home immediately, it's going to rot you know."

"I know, what I'm trying to say is, if you'd like to eat some street foods on the way home." Somewhat embarrass

"Maybe next time, let's get home, or this will stink sooner or later."

"O-Okay" Disappointed.

Gosh, she didn't have to be so rude, she could just say that she don't eat street food, I'd totally understand.

He's starting to annoy me, asking me all of a sudden if I want to eat. Lately, he's just not himself; I wonder what's happening in his head.

-17:15-

Well we're home, and it seems like she isn't going to talk with me anymore. She practically ignored me the whole way home; she didn't have to take that question seriously does she?

He seems to be affected with what I answered earlier, I wonder if I hurt his feelings in any way, though maybe he's just not used to being ignored since his popular. All popular are worshipped like god/goddesses in school. Maybe this is taking a toll in him, well that's good for him!

I can't believe she's this stubborn; it was just one simple question, nothing to be mad about. And here we go to cook, all silence. Hope she'd talk to me, I really do want to learn and I won't learn it this way.

-22:30-

It's the nth time of rolling in my bed. I can't seem to fall asleep. It's beginning to be frustrating, and yet it's a nice frustration.

** ** ** ** ** ** ** ** ** **

Cassey quietly wash the vegetable bought earlier, while looking at him from time to time to check if he's still looking.

"Hey! You could talk you know? I won't understand you just by showing that to me."

"It is better to learn watching, than talking."

"For you maybe, but for me I need to hear some instruction so I won't forget it."

"Fine, wash the vegetable like this"

"Why?"

"What do you mean why?"

"Why wash like that? Can't it be washed differently?"

"You need to wash the vegetable thoroughly, if you got other way you can do it, but this is how I wash it"

"Okay, I get it, thanks."

"You try it."

Mark, a bit surprise in her offer but still gladly accepts it. Like a child excited to venture in another world; he excitedly gets the vegetable from her hand and wash it."

Cassey, on the other hand, looks at how he's doing and slowly washes it with him."

Their hands touching, and then blushes a little. Embarrass at what they got themselves to.

"This is how you clean the fish" Showing it to him

"Can I-- Can I try?" Like a child wanted to learn more.

He tried and tried but couldn't get it right, it's his first time. She holds his hand, directing his hands in what to do and how it should be done.

"When all the ingredients are already washed and in place, we can now cut it into pieces if you like or not either way its okay, then we cook; for this time we only cut the vegetable."

Slowly showing him everything that needs to be done, and letting him try a few rounds. They started cooking, at first he got scared of the popping of oil, since she had warned him that it may leave a mark if it splash on you. Then slowly, bit by bit, he started to enjoy himself.

"What's the ginger for again?"

"To absorb the fishy aroma of the fish, so the meal would smell nice."

"Oh… That's nice."

Cassey guides him as he cooks the fish, then the vegetable. She carefully helps him not to overcook it. She helps him by pouring the ingredients and maintaining the flame and the temperature not to burn it.

Mark, on the other hand, instead of focusing all his attentions in what he's being taught he seems to be always interrupted by her guiding hand. His attentions are always diverted away from his lessons.

After the cooking lesson; Cassey sneakily open the freezer and gets an ice cream container out. Opening cabinets to look for the ice cream cone, and prepared two. Mark smiling little bit.

"Here! You deserve this for a job well done,"

"Thanks!"

"Sorry 'bout earlier, at the wet market thing"

"Oh that? It's nothing, thank you for teaching me and for this" Holding up the ice cream.

It was their moment, finally talking without arguing, just enjoying themselves.

-23:00-

Yawn I can't seem to forget what happen earlier during our cooking.
dreaming: the cooking incident

~Chapter 3: Wednesday~

-3:00-

Yawn it's three in the morning and still I can't get any decent sleep, this isn't good I have a whole day ahead of me. Maybe drinking some milk would help me go to sleep.

Yawn this is such a bothersome. I can't get any decent sleep; I kept thinking and thinking about what happened. I'll drink milk, my mom used to say milk can help you have a good night sleep, might as well give it a try. *Yawn* so bothersome.

-6:00-

Yawn I can't take this anymore, its shower for me and out for jogging.

Yawn this isn't working; I think I'll take a jog or something to take out this matter out of my head.

I didn't know jogging could be this relaxing, hope I'd be able to sort things out for this day, I can't take any chances, I can't lose my face over this bet.

Yawn jogging I go. I seem to be sleepy now that I wanted to be awake. Why should it be so bothersome? I have to wake myself up, this is another challenging day for me, can't lose the bet.

I'm starting to be so relaxed now, I think I can handle this day now. Surely, I wouldn't lose the bet, no!

Yawn I think I'd head back home and sleep for a while.

Jogging could be relaxing, but fact still remains a fact, it's very tiring, especially for me at this state, no sleep I mean. I might as well sit down in those benches to rest for a while before heading back home and prepare for school, don't want to be late or else, detention.

-8:45-

Yawn Wonder what time is—oh no! Quarter to nine! No!! I'm late! Detention!!

-9:00-

Yawn I had a great sleep, thank you. This would be a nice day, oh no! The time! I spoke too soon, it's nine already I'm so late.

-9:30-

"Nice of you two to join us" the teacher said.

Oh no! This is the first time I ever been late, this is so humiliating.

I am so dead in detention!

"Since you two missed practically the whole class, that'll be detention and a make-up class this afternoon, so I prefer that you fixed your schedule right away I don't want any conflicts with my time. That's it for the day." Fixing his things, facing up to them and said "Later five o'clock detention room"

Oh no! Not detention, I'll be in so much trouble, you got no idea how scary that old librarian is. I still remember my first day of duty during first year, I was late because of the trouble I got because of Mark Rivera, and she just didn't listen to my explanation, she practically screamed her head off. I was so scared that I never did become late ever again. She could be stricter than that especially now that I'm in my third year. Oh wait! I'm not doing my library duty, he is. He's dead! I got to do something or else he'll be in so much trouble, and I really couldn't afford that.

Oh man! Coach's going to kill me, again! He already warned me about being late again this month. This make-up class is such a bother. What seems to be her problem? She's all think mode this moment, it's just make-up class no coach is going to scre—uh-oh! She's dead! She's replacing me at the moment, oh no! I got to do something or else she's going to suffer the punishment coach

30

has in store for me. I don't want her to suffer, I must, truly must think of a way to have that make-up class move.

What if I talk to her? Nah! She wouldn't listen; she's so stubborn she doesn't listen to anyone. She's hard-headed like a spoiled brat. I'm very positive she wouldn't listen. What about our professor? Would he listen? But he seems so scary earlier. What do I do now?

She seems to be troubled, and here I am just staring at her, I couldn't do anything, actually I wouldn't. Why is it so hard to walk right towards her and ask her if she's alright? This is so frustrating, problems just suddenly pour down, after yesterday's fun.

Sigh I'm going nowhere with this thinking. I can't think anymore, wonder how he's handling it. Whoa! He seems to be taking this more seriously than I think. He shouldn't be banging his head, if he isn't all this serious. I believe he might get concussion with that successive banging, he might faint. That would be another bother for us; it'll be too hard for me. Wait! What am I thinking? I really don't care if he likes banging his head on that table. Come on Cassey focus! Let's go! You can do it! Fight!

Come on Mark, get a hold of yourself. You can't solve anything by banging your head on the table over and over again. Look at her, she's calm and collected, she's thinking about this thoroughly, be like her. Calm yourself Mark, Calm yourself. Easy Mark, easy! You can figure out something, just think how to solve it one at a time. I know you can do it. Here we go!

-12:00-

Finally! Lunch break! I got more than an hour to persuade Professor Yurman to reschedule the make-up class.

Oh no! Its lunch time already and I still haven't got any clue on what to do. I'm doomed! We're doomed! No wait! I have something, I could forfeit this bet, and then I could take on the detention and handle the punishment myself, so that he wouldn't be in so much trouble. But! I don't want to, I want to know more about his life, and I'm still enjoying those breakfast every morning. Snap it out Cassey! It's for him, stop being so selfish. Alright! I have decided, now I just have to walk to him and say that I give up.

I should hurry if I want to catch him, students aren't allowed inside faculty room during lunch time, and even if it's important they wouldn't open the door until one in the afternoon. I got to run for it!

Where is he going? Running off like that, I have to follow him. I wonder what got into him this day, ever since the word detention rang into his ears, he seems to lose himself.

Why is she following me? Is she also going to talk with Professor Yurman? That'll be great if it was the case, but what if she thought about giving up? I sure hope not, I'm still not able to know more about her, I'm still in the middle of my search. I wanted to know so much, who she is and what she is. I believe she isn't whom I see every day at school, there is something more beneath her than the surface she's showing. I wanted to know who Cassey Garcia really is, that is why I swapped lives with her to know that fact.

Why is he not stopping? He has seen me right now, he could've stop or look behind to ask me about this matter. He's obviously ignoring me; you think you could outrun me huh? Well guess again Mark, I won't lose track. You won't succeed in your plan.

Why is she so persistent? I got to run.

There he is! "Professor Yurman wait up!"

Oh come on! Look back please, I need to talk with you. Come on look back Professor Yurman. Yes!

"What is it Mr. Rivera?"

"About the make-up class sir, I want to ask you about rescheduling it."

"And why would I do that? I told you to fix your schedule, not mine."

"You don't understand you have to… You just got to."

32

What are they talking seriously about? Should I eaves drop or not? I wanted to know what it is about, but it's wrong to listen to others conversation without their permission. What am I going to do?

"So you see sir, as I have mentioned please—please reschedule the make-up class."

"Okay, but if you answer this question honestly and validly"

'I promise to answer it honestly"

"Is Ms. Garcia that important to you?"

"I-I don't really know, but as of now all I could think about is her safety from coach's justice."

"Okay, I'll accept that, then why are you always teasing her?"

"I don't know it's just that it feels so nice every morning when I hear her cursing me, I know it sounds stupid but I enjoy making her angry."

"Okay! Thank you for your honesty I'll reschedule the make-up class tomorrow, Thursday, is that fine?"

"Yes thank you! Thank you very much."

He looks happy, wonder what's happening. I feel like I'm a stalker with what I'm doing right now. It isn't really necessary to hide behind this pole is it? Why am I so afraid for them to see me? Why do I feel like I'm scared to face him? What am I feeling? I give up! I don't want to think anymore. Yes, finally, here he comes.

"Mark, we need to talk"

"Cassey, I need to tell you something first." All she could so was nod.

"The make-up class is moved tomorrow, no more worries about the activity later this afternoon."

"How did you? What happened?"

"I persuade him to reschedule it."

Eyes brightly shinning and slowly she hug him warmly whispering "thank you"

What is this feeling?

-14:30-

Why can't I forget the hug?

-15:00-

What is wrong with me? How did that happen?

-15:30-

All I could think about is that hug and that feeling

-16:00-

I got to ask her what's that about, she just couldn't hug anyone she wants when she feels like it. That was inappropriate.

Oh no! I wonder what he's thinking, about that hug. I know it's inappropriate but it was an accident, I wasn't able to contain all the excitement inside me when I heard him say that make-up is tomorrow. *Sigh* what should I do? He might ignore me after that.

But on the other hand he/she feels warm.

-16:30-

It's end of the class, a class I missed because of thinking about the hug.

-16:45-

Finally class is over. But still I'm lost with this feeling inside me, wanting to burst out.

-17:00-

I'm so not in the mood for this right now, I hope this finishes soon.

"Hey! Stop daydreaming over there and start working."

"Y-Yes of course, sorry it wouldn't happen again."

-18:30-

Finally all done; wonder how she's doing now. I better clean-up fast so I can catch up with her, and have that chat I'm anticipating. I've been thinking about what that hug could mean, could she be feeling something towards me? Yeah right she loath me, how can she possibly feel something so pleasant with me. But then what does she really feel about me anyway? I know she loath me, by the way she acted towards me, but since this swap all she did was to be kind with me, never did once she teased me like I used to do with her every morning and every time we meet. I'm so lucky that she's the one I swap lives with, if it was somebody else, I wouldn't be sure what would have happened to me right now, I might have given up already by now.

-18:40-

Finally, water break, I'm parched. Oh! Its forty past six already, it means he's all done with library duty, hope he's cleaning by now, I don't know what would happen to him if he didn't. He just got no idea how strict that old librarian is with cleanliness. She can't stand dust, and still up to now I don't know why she's so allergic in seeing dust, it's pretty normal. What?! Water break's finished already; I just got a sip or two. This coach is so persistent in winning; I can't believe he's being this heartless. Coach Turner was the best, he didn't give up on me and yet I was a big disappointment; I'm his biggest failure. I still couldn't forget it after all, how I loved basketball once, and how I tried so hard to turn my back on it. I look like a fool smiling like this, but I just couldn't forget how Coach Turner was a father to all of us, especially to me.

"Hey! Garcia, we don't have all night you know, competition is up this Saturday, we got to practice, practice and practice. Got that?"

"Yes sir got it all sir!"

Shish! So persistent; I'm not even a part of this team, I'm just replacing one of them, but that doesn't mean I'll be playing. Woman isn't allowed to play at Man's league you know!

-19:00-

Just right on time, they should be finish soon; I'll just wait here for her. I wouldn't want her to escape my curiosity; she has to answer it whatever happens. Oh yeah, it's good that I remember I have to call at home, that I'll be late, because I'll be waiting for her.

-19:25-

Why isn't she coming out yet? Could she be held up by the guys at the comfort room? But it couldn't possibly, there's a ladies room there. What seems to be the reason, I might as well go in and see for myself. What is this? They're still practicing? Its past seven already, what got into them? S-She can play? How could that be? She's a nerd! She read books all the time, carry all those heavy books all the time, she's always surrounded by books and school stuff, how could she know how to play? She—it's not her, it surely can't be her; I got to get out of here. I can't let her see me.

How could that happen? When did she learn how to play? She's a girl and yet she plays so well, as if she had a very good background of the sport. She's even smiling, seems like she's enjoying herself. She kind of looks like that player that I idolized before. I can still remember how I look up to her even if she's a woman; she's very talented and well disciplined. She always smiles during game, she plays like a child playing ball but she's very serious and determined to win every

36

time. But then all of a sudden she disappeared. And still up to now, no one still knows what happened to her and how is she now. I got to take this off my mind, I'm going home.

-19:45-

"I'm home!"

"Welcome back! Now that you're here, we can now decide what to eat."

"Excuse me?"

"We always do take outs during Wednesday, since you're new here, we'll let you decide"

"Okay, so what are the choices?"

"Chinese, Japanese, Korean, Italian, American, or Mexican"

"Chinese! I like Chinese cuisine."

"You sound like Cassandra"

"Excuse me? Who's Cassandra?"

"Cassey, who else? You think Cassey is her whole name? It's just her nickname."

"Cassandra Garcia, her name seems to be familiar."

"Of course it'll be familiar; she used to be popu—oops! I slipped; she's going to kill me"

"Of course! Cassey B. Garcia, Cassandra Bernadette Garcia, so that's what 'B' stands for, she's that famous basketball player I once idolized before—Oh wait! What did I just found out? She's—she's... No she couldn't be its not possible is it?"

"Actually you got it right, that's her whole name, when she left the sport she got her name short and let her hair grow, and she wore eyeglasses even though she didn't need one. She changed ever since that day."

How could this be? Cassey, the woman I'm always teasing, the woman whom I always do prank with is none other than my inspiration? How could that happen? How did my idol turn into a nerd? What happened to her? She used to be so—No! It couldn't possibly be her; I'm positive that it isn't true; they're just playing with me. It just couldn't be!

-20:00-

Finally practice is done for today, shish that coach is so heartless, he let us suffer practice for another hour without us noticing it. He's cruel; and yet I enjoyed myself. Like the first time I ever held a ball in my hand. It's like I'm becoming that child again, but then again (looking at her knee down to her ankle, where her previous injuries are) I couldn't be like that girl again. It just wouldn't happen again, that was my time and I've wasted it. There is no more left for me now, it's all over for me. Stop dreaming Cassey you can never be that again. You're Cassey now, not Cassandra Bernadette Garcia anymore.

-20:15-

This house sure is quiet, maybe it's time that I ask questions around here, this isn't right anymore. Where are his parents? I need to see them somehow during this swap; they shouldn't be hiding themselves from me, which is by the way rude. There he is, the ne who has been serving my meals every morning, he could be an answer, might as well as him about this situation.

"Excuse me, could you please tell me where Mark's parents are?"

"Not here I'm afraid"

"Are they hiding from me?"

"No ma'am, his father is always out of sight, he never got the chance to see his father."

"Why is that? And what about his mother, where is she?"

"I'm afraid his mother's dead, and his father work all the time, he never had the chance to bond with his son since his wife died years ago."

"You mean he never got the chance to have a whole family?"

"He did, when he was younger, but at the age of six, he has been living alone in this house, his father just sleeps here at night and as soon as he's awake he's gone."

"Oh, I see, thank you."

He's so getting a word from me; he didn't even bother mentioning it to me. He could've warned me about his parents, I could've been more prepared to face what was in front of me now. I could've done something, like wait for his father and talk with his father about him. Which is what I'm going to do tomorrow, I would have to think of the perfect plan tonight so that I'll be prepared for the near encounter, I just hope that he'll talk with me.

-22:00-

Aargh! This is going nowhere; all I could think about is what her brother told me earlier, I couldn't concentrate on studying anymore. I have a big test tomorrow, and I have to pass it, or else I'm in big trouble, she's going to get hysterical over it. Come on Mark, focus all you thoughts in this Chemistry, you got to Mark, come on.

-23:00-

I give up! I can't think of a better solution on my own, I need to ask him for help, I can't do this on my own, he's not my father anyway. That's right! Go ask him tomorrow, and everything will turn out just fine, nothing more to worry about, I can now sleep and hope for the best tomorrow.

No!! I can't take this anymore, I couldn't concentrate, and I give up! Nothing more is going to happen if I persist on it. Come what may, I really don't care about it anyways, I'll just do my best

39

and the rest is a mystery. I need to talk with her about that issue too, I want to rest assured that it's not her, it couldn't possibly be her. I have to put all this aside and sleep so I wouldn't be late again for tomorrow.

I need to find her/him or else everything wouldn't turn out just right.

~Chapter 4: Thursday~

-3:00-

What time is it? It's just three in the morning and yet I'm wide awake, I can't seem to fall asleep at all last night. I still couldn't believe what her brother told me, it seems so impossible, and yet by the looks of it, he doesn't seem to be lying either. I don't know what to think anymore. Why didn't she say something? Why did she hide things like that, she could've been more respected at our school, we could've been... I don't know close or something. If she really was Cassandra Bernadette, why did she hide? Why did she leave the sport? Why did she disappear, at the most important peak of her career? She could've done so much more if she didn't disappeared. I may still don't know the whole story but somehow I felt so betrayed, I feel so disappointed at her for doing that. She failed herself and her fans.

-3:15-

I might as well get up and run some lap to ease my mind; I'll run 'til the last drop of this emotion is out of my system. I'm getting insane with this too much thinking, it isn't like me. Ah! I almost forgot my watch like last time; don't want to be late again. And off I go to the vast horizon awaiting me.

-4:20-

I can't take this anymore! No matter how much I run, no matter how fast I get, it can't leave my mind. I couldn't stop thinking about it; his words came ringing back to my ears over and over again. Is it the truth, that's why it can't leave my mind? Or is it just that I couldn't bear it if that was the truth. I'm defeated! I'm giving this up; nothing is going to happen anymore even if I still continue thinking about it. Nothing more would've happen. Nothing will change the fact that I was hurt before and am still hurting now. I'm going back home.

-4:30-

I think I'm going to take a bath now; nothing's going to happen to me here anyways. I can still remember the day when I heard she's gone, how much I cried that night, and how much weight I have lose. But why now, that somehow I have the lead to the truth, I'm still silently crying inside.

** ** ** ** ** ** ** ** ** **

I was her number one fan, I always attend her games, use my free time to visit and watch her practice. I learned to stalk because I was very much interested to know everything she knows; I wanted so bad to play like her. But one day, she just disappeared. One by one her fans gone to another idol; one by one they forget her as if she never did exist. Until one day no one could remember her anymore. But I kept on believing, I kept hoping and waiting for her return, but she didn't. I thought if I could play like her, she'll come back, but however good I get, it wasn't enough to get her back on the court. When I finally lose hope, there she is coming out from her shadows, showing herself once more. And I couldn't take it, no rather; I wouldn't take it, I just couldn't accept it. I was hurt too much to even listen to her explain now. I can't believe that all my hard work was wasted after all, she's not whom she used to be, not anymore. Cassey is Cassey and Cassandra is Cassandra nothing's going to change it. Now that I finally know the truth, I might as well give up on her and start living on my own. Start living up my dream.

But then again, what is my dream? I only played this hard because I wanted to find her, now that I found her, where do I go from here? What path should I take now? Now that she's here, who am I then?

** ** ** ** ** ** ** ** ** **

-5:00-

Yawn It's five in the morning already? It feels like I just slept a few hours or so. Well time to get up, practice starts at six. *Yawn*

She's probably awake by this time, their practice starts at six. I'll pay her a little visit, then confront her, I'm pretty sure she wouldn't lie especially in front of the guys. She hates embarrassment, she won't back away. But what if she gets hurt, would she?

I hope practice would be light, so I wouldn't be sleepy later during class; moreover I still got detention after class. I want to be fully awake during detention, because that's the only time I will have to spend with him, I can confront him with all this questions in my mind and formulate a plan for them to be together at last.

Why do I feel so uneasy all of a sudden, I was so sure about this a while ago, but now... What happened? Why do I keep thinking that she might get hurt? What do I even care about her, she hurt me first, I shouldn't care about her feelings like she did to me and all of her other fans. Why does it seem so difficult to hurt her? I shouldn't even care about it, what is wrong with me?

Is it still appropriate for me to meddle with this thing? It's so personal already, maybe I should go ask him first about this issue then let him speak up. But what if he didn't speak up? What if he wanted it to be left as it is than do something about it. What should I do? I'm so concerned and ready about this earlier, and then now why am I feeling this way? Why am I beginning to feel guilty about all this? Would I somehow hurt him or his pride? Will he be angry at me for doing this? But I only want to help, I want him to have the family he wants, or is it what I want for him? I'm getting all confuse, might as well leave this as it is and talk about it later with him.

Sigh I give up; I'll just confront her later this afternoon during detention. There's nothing more I could do really. All I could do now is just to wait and see what would happen next.

-5:45-

Just in time! I'm safe from punishment, better wear my rubber shoes and warm up. What is he doing here? It's still early for my—rather his class this day. He seems to be looking for someone? Am I late already? But it's quarter to six; I couldn't be late, am I?

Where is she? Why isn't she here? She should've been here by now. It's a good thing I went here early, I should've known. She's a quitter. Might as well go ho—I spoke too soon, what is she doing here? Is she honestly going to join the practice this morning? Is she really playing in my place? What's happening?

Do I look like a ghost? He doesn't have to look at me like that. He probably thought that I won't go here since I'm just a substitute, well he's wrong. I'm not a quit—No, I am one. I quit without fighting once, and until now I'm still running away from it. I still can't look forward because of this, my injury or rather my insecurities. Because of this I lost everything, I lost my life. I lost myself. I lost my family. I lost a friend; there was nothing left for me anymore, because of this stupid injury, because of one stupid and simple mistake.

She looked surprise and now she's all gloomy, what's wrong with her? Do I look that bad, for her to frown that way? I can't take this expression of hers, it's so nice to see her all cheery and smiling, like she used to—Stop that Mark, she's not the same anymore, don't think of her that way. Stop thinking and just walk up to her tell her to go to practice right now or she'll be late. Come on Mark just a little bit further.

"You know, if you won't hurry you'll be late."

"Huh? Excuse me?"

"I said if you won't go there now coach will surely punish you."

"Oh, sorry I was distracted by a thought."

"Don't think about it much; well I'll be going now, good luck on your practice Cassandra."

"Yes, thank you."

"Well goodbye"

"Wait a minute; did you just call me Cassandra?"

"Umm…"

Did I say it out loud? Oh no! I'm exposed, what would I do? How would she react if she finds out that I already knew the truth? Oh no! I'm still not prepared for this.

"Maybe I just heard it wrong, so bye then I'd be going in, be careful on your way then."

"Yeah sure, bye"

I'm sure he did call me Cassandra, but he couldn't possibly know that would he? My brother promised me he wouldn't slip, or did he? My secret is exposed, this force me to do nothing more but to tell the truth. The whole truth and nothing but the truth; I think it's about time for him to know about my disappearance. He has the right to know anyway. We may not be talking with each other but I know he supports me all the way, before that incident. But what if he didn't understand? What if all this is too heavy for him to carry, would he still listen? I don't know what to think. I have to think this thoroughly before doing anything stupid; I might risk the only thing I have with him.

Oh no! I know she knows that I called her Cassandra purposely. I know that she just say that for us to forget this matter for a while, because she's going to be late. Oh no! I haven't confronted her, and I'm already hurting her like this. Why did I slip? That was stupid of me. Wait up—Hold up for just a second. I'm angry at her, no make that furious. I wanted so bad to get back at her and now all I'm thinking is how I'm hurting her? What's wrong with you Mark, you're already firm about this and now this? So what if you aren't prepared for this? That already happened so you got to confront her now! I'll just go back and—wait I can't do it now, I have classes to attend to in less than an hour, I'll just do the confrontation later at detention. I'll have my laughs later, you'll see.

I wonder what's going to happen at detention… *Sigh* my only wish now is for him to listen. *Sigh*

-6:45-

Why am I worrying so much? It's not like I did something wrong to him. Why am I feeling so guilty, especially now that he knows about whom I used to be *Sigh* I don't know what to think anymore, I'm messed up.

45

-7:15-

What is wrong with me? All I could think about is what she's going to feel afterwards when I'm supposed to be thinking about how to get back at her. This is stupid! I'm becoming so compassionate to her, when I should be furious at her. Why am I feeling like this, what's happening?

-7:45-

Finally water break, I'm parched. What am I going to do about him anyways? Since that encounter this morning I can't seem to concentrate and give it my all in this practice, my mind wanders of when cheering rings through my ear. I can't stop thinking about what's going to happen now that he knows. Why am I feeling this way, it feels like I've hurt him in some way that my mind just couldn't accept. What is wrong with me? Why do I care so much about what he's going to feel afterwards? I think that this might be the right time to tell him what happened before, no more lies, there's no use of lying anyways now that he knows, besides he have the right to know it from me, not from anybody else. I've decided this will be the day. It has to be today.

-8:15-

Stop it! You got to focus, come on Mark I know you can do it focus! You have to stop thinking about her, nothing's going to change it now, and it's already too late. Stop it now! Stop thinking about her as if something good would happen. Stop dreaming already; come on focus on your class, now deep breaths. Okay, you're doing well, inhale, exhale, and inhale, exhale, now ready for class. But she looks all-- NO-NO Stop it! Stop thinking about her! Stop it right now!

-8:45-

Wow! What has gotten into this professor, letting us go fifteen minutes early, maybe he doesn't have anything more to teach so he just let us go early to cover up his lack of preparation. *Sigh* their practice should be over soon, I think I'll drop by and see how she's doing, since I can't really take this things of my mind anyway.

-9:15-

Finally! Practice is over, I'm so tired. I want to sleep but I can't because I still have classes to attend to. I wonder how the others are handling this. Late night practice last night and now early morning practice then later on classes begins, and as of this time, I'm beginning to be sleepy.

There she is looking so sleepy, the morning practice isn't tiring at all, look at those guys they're—Huh? Why do all of them look so sleepy? Is it because of the late practice last night, or was it that the practice this morning is really hard? But coach wouldn't do that, it's just impossible, he knows we still got classes after this. What happened? How could this be? Oh no! Maybe coach is pushing them further because I wouldn't be playing with them this Saturday, no one's going to back them up during the game, and so they're being push to their limits, even farther than their limits for the upcoming game. I think this bet had got to stop now, I can't afford my team mates to get hurt, and I just can't do that. I can't live with that. I got to do something, or rather give up something.

What is he doing here? Did he come here to make fun of us, or he's worried about his place in this team. Well surely, he's still their number one player; no one is able to be like him in this team yet, so he doesn't have anything to be worried about. He's number one! I'm really sleepy *yawn* I think I'll just doze off for a few minutes in this bench, my eyes are too *yawn* tired to kee—

She's like a baby; she'll just sleep wherever she feels like it, just like that. She didn't even look if there's something there or if it'll be comfortable for her or something, she just sat and lie down. And now she's sleeping so soundly like a baby. She looks so pretty this wa— Stop thinking Mark! Stop it! She's not cute, nor is she pretty. You hate her don't you? You hate her and that's that. Don't you dare to think of something pleasant about her.

Why is he struggling *yawn* I'm so sleepy. *Yawn* I can't believe that coach is a monster; he looks nice the first day. *Yawn* I don't care whether I'll be late for my class or not, I'll get some sleep. *yawn* is he coming this way or farther away? I really can't tell, my eyes are growing *yawn* heavy...

"I'm sorry Mark, I'm sorry." Drifting off to sleep

Sorry? It's too late for a sorry! You know I hate you so much! You just got no idea how hurt I was when you left the court, and now unexpectedly when all my hopes has died down, you'll came crawling out of the shadow. I hate you! I want you out of my life! You just got no idea how much I hate you right now! *Sigh* it could have felt so good if you could only hear that, but how much I try I just couldn't bring out those words from my lips. I don't even understand myself right now for feeling this way, I wanted to shout at you or do something bad at you but I can't force myself to do it, as if I don't hate you at all. How I wanted you to know everything, but I couldn't. I just couldn't bring myself in harming you in any way possible. My system's all confused; my mind and my heart aren't really playing the same cards and I don't know why, it just felt so weird.

Look at you, sleeping like a baby, so carefree and innocent. How do you manage that? How can you even sleep? You're such a—Aargh! I couldn't even finish my sentence! I'm out of here, you're so worthless, and I can't believe I'm wasting my time here.

-12:30-

Finally lunch time! I'm so famished, I couldn't believe myself for dozing of like that, I should've alarmed my watch then somehow I could've eat something before coming to class. I'm so hungry I could eat a horse. Not that I can eat it, yuck! Just thinking about eating it disgust me, but nevertheless I'm so hungry I need food.

There she is finally; I thought this food will be put to waste. What does she thinks she's doing? Cutting line isn't a good idea you know, I got no choice then but to call her.

"Hey! Cassey! Over here." She turned around to look at the owner of the voice.

People around them turn head when Cassey started to go towards him, whispers started and they look from time to time to see whether they were dreaming or this was reality that they're seeing, the two of them together.

"Hey! Why did you call me? Do you need anything? Could this wait I'm really famished and--"Her sentence cut short when he interrupted.

"I bought you lunch, I thought you'd be hungry by now, and usually at this time it's hard to get some food"

"Oh, t-thanks" she managed to say.

Why am I doing this again? I've decided not to talk with her and to be nice at her, and yet here I am being so generous in giving her lunch. I hate myself for doing this.

"Umm… Mark thanks again for the food, and I hope you accept this, my payment." Handing over some amount of money

"No needs to pay for that really, take it as my thanks for the bread and juice the other day."

"But you brought me food last night."

"Take that as my thanks for Jacklyn's lunch the other day."

"O-Okay, thanks you so much."

And I didn't ask her to pay for it? I'm really nuts! I can't believe I'm doing this, what's wrong with me?

He seems quieter than the last time; I sure hope he's okay. I wonder what got into him. He should hate me by now, especially from the things he found out from my brother. I really don't know how to put this, but somehow I have to tell him the truth about it, but I don't know where to start. Should I just blurt it out?

"Hey, sorry about calling you Cassandra earlier"

And I'm saying sorry? I'm really nuts.

"About that, I'd like to talk about it with you"

"What about it?"

49

Well here goes nothing; we already finished lunch anyways, so it doesn't matter if I said it out right now.

"You see, my name is not Cassey, its Cassa—"

"I know I heard it from your brother, there's nothing more to say."

"Actually there is, I want you to know the truth"

"I don't care about your explanation anymore, so don't bother"

"You—you have to know the truth."

"I don't care!"

"B-But—"

"I told you I don't care! Why is it so hard for you to understand that I DON'T CARE?!" Punching the table as hard as he could, releasing every bit of his anger within his punch.

"I'm sorry." Tears building up to her eyes, trying hard not to pour it, not in front of him

"You know! I shouldn't be talking with you right now for hating you this much; you got no idea how hurt I was before. You just have no idea!"

"I know, that's why I'm apologizing now, and I wanted you to know the truth."

"I already know the truth. You're a quitter! Nothing but a quitter, you quit on me, your fans and everyone else that surrounds you, and most of all you quit on yourself. You're nothing but a worthless piece of junk!"

This time her tears came pouring down to her cheeks, she wasn't able to contain all of them in her eyes anymore; she weeps. It was just too much.

"You're wrong, I didn't quit on you. I might have given up on myself but never did I give up on you, so don't you dare tell me I quit on you." She managed to say, in between sobs.

"Yeah right! As if I would believe a loser like you?! From now on, refrain from talking or even colliding with me, after this stupid bet let's forget each other and everything that had happened. I don't want to remember someone so selfish and as worthless as you--" PAK!

She manages to slap him, tear whelming in her eyes. She looked at him with disgust for a while and started running, crying out loud, leaving him stunned at his place.

I couldn't believe him, thinking about me that way. I can't take this anymore! It's just too much to bear, how could he?! He doesn't even know anything!

How dare she slap me, she's at fault here. *Sigh* but then again, it must've been too hard for her, I have told her very harsh words that I can't imagine myself saying, especially with her. What's wrong with me? I'm not myself lately, but then to think about this thoroughly, it turn out quite better than what I expects. I have finally told her how much I hated her for doing that, and in return I have accepted the consequence. I should stop myself from thinking about her and what had happened; this isn't doing any good for me anymore.

I couldn't believe he had said all those things to me *sniff* He doesn't need to be that harsh on me; I'm not all faults here. He's so judgmental, he doesn't even know the truth and he acted like he knew everything. I know it has been hard for him when I left but it was harder for me, it was I who left that sport, it was also I who had undergone all those pain, not him. He doesn't have that much right to feel that way.

-16:45-

Sigh Detention, I wonder what would happen. I hope I won't see her; I'm not ready to face her again, especially for what had happened during lunch.

-16:55-

51

Sigh I hope my eyes won't be that obvious, I don't want to let him know I cried the whole time, I just can't bear the humiliation I'll get myself into. I just hope he would ignore me the whole time, so I wouldn't be able to face him and I'll be able to have my own little world in this room. Well here it goes, nothing more to lose.

Huh? She came? After all that had happened, she still came here, like nothing happened at all. She's supposed to be running home after that incident, but then why didn't she? She's a quitter after all, that should've been her initial reaction. But why is she here? Am I wrong about her?

He looks at me with disbelief, is he thinking that I won't go here? I hope he wouldn't notice my eyes; I would just hate it for him to see it.

Is that—is that red puffy eyes from crying? Did she cry the whole time? But why would she? Nah! Maybe she just wants me to pity her so I'll say that I'm sorry for saying all those harsh words at her, I'm not that stupid you know! I won't fall for your tricks.

I hope detention would go by quickly.

-19:45-

"I'm home, sorry about being late, I promise to do the kitchen duty tomorrow."

"Have you eaten already?" Asked her brother

"Yeah, thanks, I'm going to the room now."

Finally a time on my own, no one to bug me or something, *sigh* I'll lie down for a while—oops. What's this? I know I shouldn't intrude something so personal but—Aargh never mind it's just a simple notebook, it wouldn't be that personal. It looks like her notes, let see the last entry.

He did a good job this championship game; he has improved a lot since high school days. If this keeps up, he sure got the edge in becoming a NBA player, like he dreams of, or so I thought. I

52

really don't know he's dream, we really never got the chance to talk. The day I finally decided to talk with him, still until this day remains a dream. And will be nothing more than a dream

What's this? I can't understand this, what is that girl thinking, writing something like this? She's such a weirdo. What are these pictures, enclosed in this notebook? Hmm… N-No way! This is me, from the bench line during her games, and this one is from their practice session and this one too, and this too. Huh? What's this empty bench? What's this fo—T-That's my usual place during her games, what does this mean? Is there's something written on the back. Let me--

Today's the big day! Championship, my chance in entering a good university and playing college ball, my dreams of becoming one of those WNBA players I admire so much is coming nearer. This day would be even greater because I've finally decided to talk with him and ask him to join us in the celebration later that is if we won. But all my dreams came crumbling down after…

The message isn't complete, where's the next o—W-What's this? When did this happen? When did she break her leg? There's also something at the back.

Just like that, my dreams came crumbling down before my very eyes. That was stupid of me, forcing that drive and all, I could've just faked it but I didn't I chose to lay-up that ball, and this is what happened after. How am I supposed to face him now? What would I tell him? How would I ever play again? This is my end… I'm not worth it anymore, I'm trash!

She couldn't be, could she? I know she disappeared after that championship match that I wasn't able to watch because of my own game that time, but I never did thought or even heard about her being injured and all that. How did that happened, without me even knowing it?

"You know, reading people's diary without their permission isn't nice"

"Oh, I'm sorry, I didn't mean to peek at it, it just---"

"I know, I saw the whole thing, and I know what you're thinking right now."

"When did this happen?"

53

"During the championship game, she fell down during her lay-up, hitting the floor with her knee first, with her opponent who fell on top of her leg so, as you can see she broke her leg at that time, and since then everything changed around her. She wasn't the same as before."

"What do you mean? Aside from those disguise"

"She isolated herself from all of us, she started to hate herself and the people around her, and we started to grow apart, as a family I mean."

"You seem to be close to me"

"That what everybody thinks, but they don't know that through this wall, she isn't who she used to be. She started to work for the school to avail the scholarship that she could've gotten from being in the team, but wasn't able to. She thinks that our parents are blaming her for everything that had happened. It's just too complicated to talk about it really, but the main point is, we aren't like this before, and I'm missing my sister madly already."

"I'm sorry; I got the point, no need to further expound it. I'm sorry, if I only knew, I would've refrained myself from saying those things at her, she was right I am a jerk!"

"No need to say you're sorry, it was also a good thing to make her cry like that, she's been piling up all those inside her, at least let her have the day to cry it all out. Besides, because of you, she started to stand up bit by bit, when she found out you're in the team, she quietly rooted for you, like you did during her time. She was herself when she sees you play, so thank you."

"You don't have any idea, how I made her cry. Besides I only played that hard because I was hoping that by improving more and more I could make her come out again and play once more, but it never did came. And now I knew I'm so sorry about what I have done earlier this day.

I'm such a jerk; she was trying to tell me what really happened. So that's what she meant when she told me 'I didn't give up on you' I should've known. I'm such a stupid jerk, I can't believe myself. Stupid!

-22:00-

54

I can't believe this *sniff* I couldn't believe he thinks of me that way * sniff* how could he.

Hugging the pillow tightly crying her heart out, when suddenly the creaking of the door was heard.

"Are you alright?" A deep voice sounds concerned ask, a voice she never heard from this household.

She sits upright and seeks the owner of the voice.

"Who are you? What did my son do to you?"

"I'm Cassey, I'm a frie—actually your son hates me now more than ever. I'm sorry, your son and I made a bet to swap lives for a week so I'm here. Sorry about all this, I promise to clean this up, promise."

"So Cassey, what are you crying about? Could I be a father to you at this moment or rather a friend if you want?"

"Why? You aren't always there for your son, and you want to be a father to me?"

"You don't understand, he looks just like his mother, it's too painful for me to see him, and he reminds me so much about his mom, I know it must've been so long but I still do miss her."

"I'm sorry, is that why you rather spent your time at work that to bond with him?"

"Yes. Exactly! It has been hard not just for me but mostly on his part. He lost his mother at a very young age, and soon after he lost his father as well. I just couldn't bear looking at him, it hurts me too much."

"He's your son, sooner or later you have to face him whatever the cost would be, beside he looks like your wife, isn't it all the more reason to love him and care for him more? Your wife would like that, I believe."

"You're still young, you can't understand how adults feel."

"I may not know, but I understand Mark's feelings, and he really needs a father, you're all that he has left. I know that you might think that it's a little too late but there's still time for the both of you, love is never too late."

"You're funny you know? You remind me about my wife." Laughing half-heartedly

"You see, nothing's wrong" Smiling brightly

"Excuse me?" All confused at the sudden statement

"You just told me I remind you of your wife, but nothing happened, that means you can look at Mark without anything happening at all. I know you can do it, he is your son after all."

"Maybe. Maybe you're right. Well enough about me how are you?"

"Pretty much fine thank you, I felt much better. Sorry to bother you like this sir." Slightly embarrassed

"Nothing to thank of, it should be I thanking you. It's late, you better go to sleep."

"Thank you again sir, good night."

"Sweet dreams." Leaving the room thoughtfully

-22:30-

I wonder if he's dad is thinking about it seriously, I sure hope so. That way at least Mark could say that I have done something good in his life, I hope in that way he might find it in his heart to forgive me. I hope that when this life swapping ends; he'd go home smiling because his dad will be the one waiting for him.

I hope she's sleeping by now, I also hope that she's done crying. I don't want to see that red puffy eyes like earlier. I felt so guilty about everything that I have told her, I shouldn't have said all those things at her. It's not her fault anyways, she didn't do anything wrong. I'm so stubborn to even listen. This is the consequence I get.

Nothing to think anymore and I'm tired of crying, I think I might be able to sleep by now. Oh Lord please let me sleep peacefully.

Aargh! I'm stupid! I should say that I'm sorry tomorrow, whatever happens I should apologized to her, and I should repay her for the damage that I've done. I'm so sorry Cassey, I hope that you can find it in your heart ever to forgive me, I'm sorry. It's twenty to eleven, I better get some sleep, or else I wouldn't be able to think straight tomorrow. I have to make things better tomorrow. *Yawn* I have to make things bet---

~Chapter 5: Friday~

-3:30-

Yawn I better get up and fix this, it's already difficult to breath with this clogged nose. I can't believe I cried myself to sleep with such matter. But it felt god somehow, because I was finally able to cry it all out. Pouring my heart out; it was already too heavy to begin with, and with that extra load, I broke down.

I want to lie down and sleep some more but I feel like it's not necessary anymore. I think I'll make breakfast for a change, at least I could offer them something for being nice with me and all that. And maybe I'll invite Mr. Rivera to come and join us in breakfast; it could be a good start for him, so that when Mark returns his well-adjusted to the setting. Mark would be pleased about this, I hope.

I can't find the kitchen, it's the third mistake already, if this was baseball I'm strike out, off the field I go. It has already been five days since I started living here, and I didn't even bother to look around, this is so stupid of me. I think I'll start from the beginning, and this time I'll remember each room I go.

Finally the kitchen! I've found it at last! Wow! This look amazing, it's sparkling clean. I can't believe such kitchen exists; our kitchen is nothing compared to this one. I can't believe I'll be cooking here, dream come true, that is if I dream of becoming a chef which I'm not. So cooking I'll do as I planned.

-5:00-

"Is someone there?" A sleepy somewhat scared deep voice ask

"Oh, yes, it's me Cassey" she answered with a cheery voice.

"What are you doing? You aren't supposed to do kitchen works."

58

"It's okay; I'm used to it at home, nothing to worry about. Besides I'd like to offer this to all of you for being so nice, and for welcoming me here even though I'm a stranger." Smiling warmly

"Okay, if that is your wish, may I be of any assistance?"

"If you want to, yeah sure, thanks"

-5:30-

Yawn I better get up or I'll be late for my classes, I can't believe I wasn't able to sleep well last night, I'm still so tired. I better fix my bed before someone comes in, this is humiliating, the bed looks like kids played here the whole night. I should've been still, I shouldn't have rolled or tossed myself from left to right and back, and then it could've been neater. I wonder how's she doing right now, is she awake now? Is she still alright after yesterday's argument? I hope so.

Wow! I can't believe such breakfast exists. It was nice working with him; working with an expert sure is fun especially the learning stuff. I'll try my hardest to make this dish back home after this swap; I just hope that it'll taste like this. I'm very lucky at this swap, I learned a few things, and I get to enjoy luxurious things but then through this I've experience the heart aches I didn't wish to return to. Oh no! It's five thirty, I have to wash myself up and prepare for school, and I also got to ask him if he could wake Mr. Rivera and join us in breakfast. This would be great, at least the start of this day is worth smiling for, hope it'll last the whole day, but I doubt it.

"Breakfast is ready." A deep voice declared

"Finally I'm starved, let's all dig in." A cheery sweet voice answered

"The food is great, who made this?" Sincerely ask by Mr. Rivera

"Cassey and I made it, sir." The butler answered politely.

Cassey smiled and protest in a very shy tone "Your butler made it, I helped a little, though I know I wasn't any real help because he made most of it, I just hand over the ingredients and mix some."

"Thank you" Mr. Rivera smiled sincerely, and then left the table soon after he finished his meal.

Thank you? I wonder what that was for. I only did a little help, it wasn't I who made all this, besides it's very evident in the taste, I couldn't do something this great. Is it because of last night? But I didn't do anything for him, I just listened, he was the one who had done so much for me, he comforted me even though I'm a stranger and a trespasser; nothing to thank me for; it is I who needs to thank him. Oh no! I'm going to be late; I better hurry up or else I wouldn't be able to enter the room.

-7:00-

Where is that woman? She's so late, she knew we have a big test today, and our professor is very strict about time during test. Where is she? Is she planning on not going to school after what happened yesterday? Is she still crying her heart out? I sure hope not, I won't forgive myself if that was the case. A few more minutes and our professor will arrive, what time does she plan to get in class?

Oh no, I'm so late, I hope the professor isn't there yet. Is this what I get from getting up early? If that is the case, then I wouldn't like to get up early ever again. Today's the big test; I can't believe I'm going to be late. Oh no! People would really start to spread stupid rumors about me; gossips will fly throughout the school for what had happened yesterday. I'm also positive that if I didn't get there in time they'll think I'm too humiliated to even come to school or they'll think that I'm still crying over this small matter. I have to prove them wrong, I just need to get—oh no! There he is I have to get there first. Oh no you won't, I'd make it! I just got to—huff! Safe! I scored! This is kind of humiliating though, running like that and beating the professor into going in first, but at least I made it, and that is what's important as of now.

She's incredible, I can't believe she'll make it, just a split second away. Thank God she beat him, or else she wouldn't be able to take the test, she got to adjust her schedule with him for her to take that exam. And his schedule is like a jungle, unorganized for a professional like him. Now, I just hope that he wouldn't count that as a late, and I hope that she wouldn't be in any trouble; with that look on him anything is possible. I just hope that she'll be safe whatever happens. I hope she'll have that smiling face for the rest of the day.

Sigh Thank God I'm not in trouble, that was so reckless of me running like that and beating him to the door. I thought I'm a goner. I am lucky this time. Another new reason to smile, hope this will last; I don't want to cry again, my eyes still hurts a lot. I just hope that this smile will not fade from my face for the remaining time of this day; I really want to forget every heart aches and pain from yesterday. Yesterday had ended last night; today's a new day, a new beginning to start with.

-8:00-

Sigh I thought that smile would really last, but it seems that this isn't really my day. I lost my smile the minute I got my paper, written in bold red '-10'; it was a 60 item quiz and the passing is 36, I can only afford to have 14 mistakes, and the test was hell. My brain melted the second I started the test. Question number one was already difficult, guess how much more difficult it is for the following question; it seems so impossible to even pass that test. But then again, I couldn't care much at this moment; there are bigger things to set my mind with than this one, it's just a minor problem anyway, besides it isn't my grade. Or is it?

There she is again looking all gloomy, and here I am again doing nothing but stare at her. She looks so weak and fragile, and I couldn't bear more if I would hurt her again. I just couldn't make myself to walk towards her and talk with her about things. I wanted to let her know that I already know the whole truth and I'm willing to pay the consequence she has in store for me, as long as she forgives me after. How I wish that I could have some more time to finish this struggle and walk up to her but I don't, I still have laboratory duty, which is why I'm going now. Don't want to be late on the last day of my duty as a working student.

Somehow, I'm starting to regret this swap. If it wasn't for the swap he wouldn't know my secret, and I wouldn't cry, and most of all I won't be in too much pain right now. I was happy the way I am before the swap, I don't have any plans on going back to my old life anytime soon. I'm contented already with this lifestyle, three long years of being like this, I'm glad I still live, but the best part is though I'm really not enjoying it, I learned to appreciate it, for I was invincible, no one could ever hurt me, no one is expecting anything from me, I learned to live on my own; for my own and not for anyone else's expense. But now things are different, I'm out of my shadows and I'm easy to penetrate. I'm already at the verge of my existence.

What could have happened if I didn't initiate this bet? Would her secret be revealed? Would she cry to herself like that? There's so many question in mind but the most important of all is; would she still walk out of her shadows just like what had happened? *Sigh* however hard I think I know I wouldn't find any answer, because it was not me who hide all those years, and I haven't really been hiding so I guess I wouldn't know how she felt that time, and throughout those years. Now I finally realized that I am truly one heck of a jerk. That was stupid of me. Somehow I'm starting to regret this bet, I shouldn't have started it, and then maybe, just maybe I could've saved her from the pain she's in right now.

If it wasn't for this bet, I might not be able to face my fears like I'm doing right now. If it wasn't for this bet he might still have that huge gap with his father. If it wasn't for this bet, I couldn't have understood him like I understand him now. If it wasn't for this bet then maybe, I wouldn't learn this valuable lesson that I have learned. My family is the greatest gift of all.

If it wasn't for the bet, I might not learn the truth; I might have lost hope and let time withers the memories. If it wasn't for the bet, I wouldn't be able to understand her right now, nor would I even try. If it wasn't for the bet, I wouldn't understand what parent's role is to our life, finally time is coming near. I know that the right time will come, for us to finally sort things between us. And most of all if it wasn't for the bet I wouldn't grow as a person, and as a child, then I wouldn't be able to realize who I am and what am I to the others. I wouldn't have this vast horizon awaiting for me, as I go each step of the way, I finally knew my purpose.

-12:00-

Lunch time! But it isn't like any lunch time that I craved of foods, this time I crave for some peace and quiet. I really don't have any appetite right now, might as well spend the rest of the break time at the park for tranquility. I hope no one is there at this time of day; I really need some time alone.

Sigh Lunch break for an hour and off I go to my laboratory duty. Then end day of my time being a working student. The only time I got to talk with her is later at their practice during my interview time, which I'm somehow very reluctant to go to. *Sigh* I really need some time to think this over. Maybe I'll just go to my favorite part of the school, there I could think peacefully, without stress and pressure just peace and serenity embracing me.

Great! Just what I needed a place of peace and quiet, a time for myself. Finally, the park all to myself *Sigh* I know I should be grateful, but this is such a burden. It's just too much.

Great! Someone got in here first, *sigh* but what could I do anyway? There's no more turning back for me; I just have to bear sharing the park with her. I was really hoping for peace on my own but—is it-- Is it really Cassey? What is she doing here at this time of day?

Sigh whoa! What is he doing here? Is he also not eating lunch?

Oh no! She noticed me, what should I do? Should I hide? Should I turn my back and leave? I'm not ready to face her yet, especially what happened yesterday, what if she hasn't calm down yet? What am I to do?

Sigh I guess I better leave, seeing him is too much to bear already, and talking with him? I'm not so sure. I'm still hurting inside, and my tears are threatening to fall. I had to escape this before something worse would happen. I can't bear for another burden on my shoulder right now.

She's leaving, No! I had to stop her, we need to talk. But—Aargh! Never mind! I don't care anymore; all I care now is about us. About everything that had happened between us.

"Cassey! Wait up!"

"W-what?" Turning her back to see if she isn't really dreaming

"We need to talk, about what happened yesterday." Looking all concerned

Oh no! He does it, my tears—I can't contain them no! I can't *sniff* cry.

"No! Cassey no, please don't cry." Trying to hug her and let her cry on his arms

She's really hurt, she's still crying up until now. It must've been so hard for her, keeping all this feelings inside of her for the longest time. I was a jerk for ever thinking that I was hurt the most and I didn't even consider her feelings over this whole mater, all I cared about was myself, I'm not just a jerk but I'm a selfish one too.

"I-- *sniff* I'm sorry *sniff* I'm so sorry *sob*" Crying her heart out

"No, I should be the one who should say I'm sorry, if it wasn't for me, you wouldn't be in this too much pain, and you wouldn't be crying like this." Trying to calm her down, but all his efforts is ignored, she just cried more and more with the passing minute.

"I'm sorry, I said harsh words yesterday that I don't really mean, I thought that you just quit, that you ran away, I was really hurt and I don't know what to think anymore, but last night I happened to find out the truth and I know it's my fault. I didn't know that you were badly injured and—and—I'm sorry, please Cassey please don't cry."

It lasted for quite a while before she regains her posture, and cried the last drop of her tear. At that moment all he could do was to hold her tight in his arms and whisper 'please stop crying'.

"I'm sorry, for doing this to your shirt, I promise to wash it."

"Don't mind the shirt; it isn't as important as you. Are you alright?" Looking all concern

"Yes, very much; thank you, for letting me cry like that." Smiling with gratitude

"I'm sorry for hiding this long; I just couldn't get myself to say it to you after the first time."

"The first time?" He raised a brow.

"Yeah, the first time; remember the first time we ever met? I was about to talk to you about it but you made fun of me." Reminding him of what happened the first day of their first year.

"I really don't remember."

64

"Let me remind you."

** ** ** ** ** ** ** ** ** **

I was so excited when I found out that we'd be going the same school, and I really prepared for it. I wore my lucky shirt, my best jeans, my best accessories, and I even prepared a speech just for that special day. I really wanted to talk to you about everything, I wanted us to be friends, but the moment I approached you and said 'Hi can we talk?' You humiliated me by turning your back on me as if you never heard me.

The next day of school, I saw you with your new friends, and decided to just walk away when you yelled my name. I was so stunned and I didn't know what to do, I was so freak out that I forgot my prepared speech and all I could do was say 'Sorry, you mistook me with somebody else, my name's Cassey by the way.' And then I run off, as far as my leg could go, which is about three meters I think, my leg wasn't that fully healed that time, so I couldn't really run. And you made fun of it, and after that you started making fun of me. I lose the confidence to tell you, and decided to just be contented with what we have at that time, at least you notice me; that's what I thought.

And then finally, I got the job for sports news, I got the opportunity to talk with you as a student, not as a prey. That was how it all started and ended.

** ** ** ** ** ** ** ** ** **

"Oh yeah! I remember that. Sorry about that"

"It's nothing really; you aren't the only one who does that stuff on me."

"Could I ask something?"

"Shoot!" Anticipating the next sentence

"Is it you? Who post all of those notes at my locker?" Hoping the answer to be yes

"Yes, it is me. I thought that I'd be your number one fan like you are to me during my time."

"Thanks a lot for those, I really appreciate it. And just to let you know I followed the tips you taught me and I really take it to heart."

"Then it is me who should be the one thanking you."

"*Laughs* Thank you very much Cassey" Giving her a warm big hug

I can't believe it's really her, who put all of those, my secret treasure. All of my college life as a basketball player, I knew I wouldn't be this good if it weren't for her. If it wasn't for her disappearance or her notes, I wouldn't play this game with all of my heart. It was her who taught me that basketball is more than what it seems.

It felt so warm and fuzzy; I couldn't believe I finally told him everything. I'm more than happy to find out his reaction, as a positive one. If this would be a dream, I wouldn't care if I won't wake up anymore. I like it more this way, me being free from all the pain, and the sufferings, and him soaring high like an eagle.

I could finally express all that I feel, just for a moment, everything's exposed.

-15:30-

Finally, laboratory duty's over. My duties as a student volunteer are officially over, as of this day. Now I'd start my responsibility being a part of the sport news, I got too much time to prepare for everything, starting in what to interview, and how to interview it.

His work is probably done by now, and my class is soon over. I hope he remembers the interview day, I forgot to remind him about that. *Sigh* I sure hope he planned for it already, it'll be such a bother if he would still ask me about it, and it's not fair, he should do it on his own, I already helped him a lot with that draft.

-15:56-

Finally over! I've finally manage to finish the interview questions and the drafts for the news. Thanks to her prepared temporary draft. I have four more minutes before her class ends; I hope I can still catch her. I really want to fetch her from class, to repay for everything that she had done for me. I just hope she wouldn't ignore me, and accept this little gratitude of mine.

-16:00-

Yawn finally the class is over, no wonder he's failing this subject, as time passes by the teacher gets boring. Well it's time, the last day of practice this week, and tomorrow's the last day of me being a player, and then Sunday comes along, the last day of the swap, and I would be free. Free as a bird once again.

Sigh I just got here on time, thank God. There she is right now, about to leave her seat. I might as well let her know that I'm here. Now let's see if she can see me and my big wave.

What is he doing here? And what is he up to?

She notices. She really have sharp eyes * laughs*

"What are you doing here? You're supposed to be at the office" Eyeing him with one brow raise.

"Well, I'm here to fetch you, and walk you to the gym"

"And why is that?" Curiosity overcoming her

"I just want to do something for you for a change, so shall we?" Extending his arms

"Okay, if that's what you want. Let's go then" Smiling at him brightly

Whispers and murmurs are heard at their background while each and every student that walks out the room and the rooms close-by is eyeing them, expecting something to happen just like yesterday at the cafeteria, but none came.

-16:10-

"Thanks for walking with me"

"Nothing to thank for actually; I have interviews to do here too, remember?"

"Well, I'll leave you then, in your interview *laughs*"

I can't believe all this is happening, we hated each other just yesterday, and now we acted like we were best friends for the longest time now.

It's good to hear her laugh like that, it's really heartwarming. I hope that I could still here that, even after this bet. I want to see her smile more and more each day, even now that her old life is catching up on her.

-18:25-

Their practice sure is fun to watch, but I guess it would be much more fun to actually play with them. She's truly incredible; she managed to let her team mates trust her in just a short time. She has managed to be the heart of this team, even though she's just a substitute and she wouldn't be playing at the game at all. She's the same as before, nothing did changed, just her physical appearance.

Why is he smiling like that? He looks like an idiot. Well never mind him; I really don't care about what he's up to anyway. What matters now are that it is clear to all of them that I wouldn't be playing they just have to depend on themselves and not to depend on others like what they're doing.

"Cassey, borrow Mark's jersey, you'll be playing tomorrow with us."

"Sir? You aren't serious are you?" Looking at him wide eyed

"Do I look like I'm joking? I already talk with the officials and they all agreed."

"*Gulp* I'll borrow his jersey right away, excuse me." Almost running towards him

"He wants me to play, let me borrow your jersey, his orders." Not wanting to look behind her

Again I spoke too soon, what would happen to her?

"He isn't serious right?" Wanting her to say yes

"Nope, he told us, he had already talked with the officials and they said okay."

What is he thinking? Is he risking her? But that couldn't be, knowing his personality that might not be it. But whatever it is I trust his judgment completely. He always do things that would be the best for all of us, he probably thinks it could do her some benefits.

"Well, we should just trust him. You're at my house right? Just take it from my drawer, if you can't find it ask anyone to help you, and don't forget to wash it after okay?"

"Okay, thanks. And I'm sorry about all this."

"Not your fault, no need to say you're sorry."

"But still—I'm sorry"

"Well I'd be going now. Be careful on your way home okay?" Concern filling his voice

"Yes, of course, you too be careful" Smiling brightly as ever.

-19:40-

He's not really serious about this is he? But Mark told me to just trust him about this. I'm really at lost because of this entire announcement. Well, I've prepared the bag anyways, and it seems that I got everything. I might as well rest for a while, before doing anything else.

69

What could have been his reasons? It doesn't seem that he's doing this for an advantage, or is he? But he never plays that way, he plays fair and square, he doesn't like any advantages at hand. What could have been his plans? Might as well forget about it and start packing the things I will need tomorrow.

Could I play? What if that happens again? I couldn't bear to go through that pain again. I just couldn't.

Wonder what she's doing right now. Is she preparing herself, or is she thinking whether to show up or not. If I would be her, I would think this thoroughly before making any decision, and in the end I'd definitely follow what my heart is telling me. And my heart tells me she'll be playing.

It's so difficult to think about all this, should I just tell them or I would rather risk everything? I'm so lost. And this isn't supposed to happen, if I didn't play like that, none of this would've happened. I should've contained all the excitement and all the feelings that pour on me when I started to hold that ball. I just loved the game so much, and I've missed it, my heart and my soul couldn't forget it like what my mind tells me to do.

-20:45-

I better do something for her, just like she does during my games like this. Post-it wouldn't be original, so as the apples, and most of all cheering for her wouldn't be enough. I have to think of something, to cheer her up and let her know that I'm still her number one fan. That I'll be cheering for her at the bleachers and most of all is that I'm here just for her. I better start doing something, it's already late, and the game starts early

-21:30-

"Tomorrow's the big game huh?"

"Yes, and I'm really nervous about it."

"It shows, no need telling me about it."

70

"Sorry. It's just that it has been a long time since I last played."

"Stop thinking about it, it'll be too much of a pressure, think of it as you're only in practices."

"Then I wouldn't play my all."

"Won't you? Even it's just practice you have to do your very best so you'd do great in games, you'll be able to give not just your all but beyond everything."

"True, but it's nothing like the practice, there's crowd and—"

"You've overcome that before, I know you could do it again."

"I don't know…"

"The best thing to do now is sleep and gets as much rest you could get so you'd do great tomorrow."

"Thanks, good night"

"Good night, sleep tight, and believe in yourself."

"Thank you so much for everything, for believing in me like always"

"Nothing to thank for, it is my job anyways."

"True, but I still want to thank you from the bottom of my heart. Thanks for being always there for me; in both joys and pain."

"You're very much welcome, go to sleep now, okay?"

"You too, good night."

-22:00-

"*Sniff* I can't take this pain! No! It's all happening again NO!!"

Sobbing It was just a dream, only a dream. Nothing to be scared about; it was just a stupid dream. It'll never happen. It was just a dream.

~Chapter 6: Saturday~

-2:45-

I couldn't sleep anymore, I can't take this off my mind, and I think my mind would explode any minute now. Why is it so difficult to remove it from my mind, for me to relax a bit, I have a big game later and here I am struggling to get some sleep. I can't take this anymore! This is too much! I'm getting up, I don't care how early it is, and I'm taking a bath.

-3:20-

Walking through this dark empty street made me feel alone and longing for a companion, but I know it's impossible to happen. I might as well walk through this alone, with the silence as my only companion for this morning. *Sigh* Walking alone could be really lonely sometimes, especially when we are accustomed of having a companion, but I know I needed this time alone, to think, to prepare and most especially to look inside me and ask the hardest question of all 'why?'.

I often look at the mirror and ask 'why did it turn out like this?' 'Why did this happen?' 'Why of all people I should be the one who had to suffer all of this?' all the questions that was beginning with why keeps popping out in my head, and still up to this moment I can't seems to answer, not even one question I had in mind. All I could do was think and then some time later poof! As if I never thought about it in the first place. But then a part of me still longs to find it, what if all this didn't happened? Would it still be the same as before? Or rather, would it be better than before?

The clock is ticking and I'm still lost in my mind, I don't know what to do or what to think anymore, all that comes into my mind is that I'm afraid of something so unclear and unfamiliar to me, and with the reason, that I do not know of. As I sit here in the center of my stadium, I do nothing but think and hear all the foot-steps that this floor had encountered and the sound of the ball that had bounced through this floor. All I could do was to reminisce through my past and my near future.

"I thought you'd be here at this time of hour." A deep voice said out of the darkness that fills the room.

"That voice sounds familiar, have we met sir?" She answered in a shy tone

"Have you forgotten my voice Cassandra?" The deep voice answer with a silent laugh

"Coach Turner! I couldn't believe it's you, what brings you here? Where are you by the way?" She fondly answers with excitement filling her voice.

"I'm here beside you, or so I hope. I need to speak with you" he answered filling his voice with concern

"About what? Is it about this thing?" She answered in a sad tone.

"What are you so afraid of Cassandra?"

"A-afraid? Afraid of what?" She looks down, letting her hair cover her face

"Stop running away Cassandra, it'll be such a waste." He said concern

"But I am not" Looking down low as possible

"Cassandra, stop it. Stop denying everything, I know it hurts but there will come a time that you have to forget in order for you to face the new chapter of your life."

"B-but I'm not. I really don't know what you're talking about." Trying to change the topic

"Yes you do. You know exactly what I mean, why are you doing this to yourself?"

"What do you mean? I'm not doing anything."

"When will you ever stop being so unfair?"

74

"B-but I'm not. I'm not unfair."

"Are you positive about that? You're not just unfair to everyone who believes in you, you're also unfair to yourself. When will you listen to what your heart has been crying all this time? When will you?"

"I didn't ask for them to believe in me, they did that on their own, it's not my fault, and I am not being unfair not to myself nor to anyone around me."

"You used to be the team's heart; you used to be that special heart."

"What do you mean? I don't understand what heart are you talking about?"

"You were their heart, they listen to you, they play with you and most importantly you lead them perfectly, because you lead them with a heart not with a fist. What happened to that heart I knew of?"

"That Cassandra was long gone, I'm known as Cassey now and as far that I know of, Cassandra and Cassey are two different people." Trying to hold back the tears that are threatening to fall

"So I see, it seems that you've decided. There is no use for me to persuade you anymore." Disappointment filling his voice, he stands up and turn his back on her.

"I hope that you wouldn't regret this, I wish for your heart's happiness. Farewell Cassandra." He then leaves, and the sound of his shoes creaking to the floor slowly fades.

She wept.

Why is it so hard? Why can't people just accept the fact that I'm not whom I used to be? They expect too much from me, that they don't even consider my feelings anymore. Don't I have the right? Don't I have any choice? I'm the one hurting here, not them. I'm the most disappointed and affected with this situation and yet they act like they lose a world. It was me who lose everything, not them.

Just because they believed in me, and still are means that they have the power to direct me, they don't have even the slightest right to judge me or to condemned me, I was the one who was hurt. I am the one who is still hurting right at this point. And I am the one who has been bearing it all. Only I have the right to decide, the right to-- *sniff* It's just simply too much.

"Sh... Sh... I know what you feel; I know that it hurts so much."

"C-coach Turner? What are you doing here? I thought you left already?"

"Yes, but I walk right back in, I wanted to know if you still feel the same way about this game as before."

"Why? Why?" Was all she was able to say as she weeps harder.

"I know it hurts, I know how you feel, and I've been through that same situation before. I've gotten myself in that same situation before, it took me ten long years to finally realize that I was regretting all that had happened, that I shouldn't have quit before. That is why I became a coach, even though I had a good job with good pay before. I left those because this is where my heart belongs, and as a second father to you, I don't want you to take that same mistake that I did before, you still got this chance to play."

She looks at him intently, as if the dark is giving away his sad eyes that are looking in her eyes filling with concern. She tries to speak but nothing came out.   .

"You may end up falling again, but there is always a chance to stand back up and fight. Remember what I always tell you? As long as there's time on the clock—"

"You shouldn't give up, even if they lead a hundred points you can still make it if you try and fight 'til the end" She says in between sobs.

"Exactly, there is still time in your clock, why are you giving up this fight? I believe no make that I know that you can do it. I know you'll stand right back up and fight 'til the end."

"B-But I can't, what if—"

"What if what? Don't live in what ifs Cassandra, you'd regret it. So what if? You can still make it, believe in yourself once more and you'll see that miracle that has been long waiting for you."

"I'm scared." She cries

"It's okay to be afraid, but that's not the end of it, you got to look at the end, or you'll never cross that line because you were too afraid to even look at it."

"B-but... I don't know if I could still make it like before."

"No one is expecting you to be like yourself before. It takes a long time, I know, but you have to take the first step to even considering in finishing this race."

"I can't. I'm all alone, I can't make it. It's not the same as before."

"You are not alone, and you'll always not be. We are always here beside you, waiting for you to stand back up again, that we may support you all throughout this. Everyone still believes in you, so never think that you're all alone."

"Really?" Trying to stop her crying

"Yes, really. Now stand up and clean yourself up, you have a big game waiting for you."

"Y-yes!" Wiping her tears sniffing, she tries a weak smile and began to cheer herself up.

So this is how it feels when people believe in you. To have someone beside you catching you fall and helping you get back at your feet. Someone to watch over you, and exchange smiles and tears with you. So this is how it feels to be loved.

-7:30-

Yawn this is the big day! Finally the moment has come for her to shine once more. It has been a long time since she had left the limelight, she deserves this second chance, and I just hope people would give it to her easily. I sure hope that everything would turn out good. This is my day to become her number one fan again, time to prepare my 'fan thing'.

-8:15-

I'm all set to go; I got my 'fan thing'. Let me check once more; I have here her towel, energy drink, banana, and a glass of milk. I sure hope that this is okay, I couldn't think of anything better. Oh and here's my note as well. Off I go.

The big game is about to start a few minutes from now, and I still couldn't get a sight of him, did he forget? I hope not. Where is he anyways, he promised me he'll remain to be my number one fan, why is he still not here?

-8:40-

Where is he? I still couldn't get a sight of him. *Sigh* this waiting is getting hopeless; the huddle will start any minutes now. Wait! There he is *sigh* I thought he'll never make it.

"Sorry about that, this 'fan thing' took me a lot of time."

"Fan thing? What is that?" Looking at him with one brow raise

"Here, a little something just for you." Handing her the bag

"Thank you" Smiling warmly.

"Ms. Garcia, huddle time." A deep voice ordered.

"Yes sir!" Bidding him farewell

I wonder what's inside this bag. *Laughs* He is truly one amazing fan, never thought of it. Might as well eat this banana and drink this milk now, so it'll have an effect later at the game. He's truly one amazing guy. Coach Turner is right, they are still here beside me, and I'm not alone.

Smiles seems like she likes it. I sure hope she does, I thought of that all night long, my effort is paid in full. Hope that at some how I made it clear to her that I'm right here for her, she won't be alone playing anymore, well not this time. I'm now here, cheering for her like I used to be.

** ** ** ** ** ** ** ** ** **

Let me introduce you to Ms. Cassandra Bernadette Garcia, and she will be playing with us in this game. I want you all to work together as a team. I want each and every one of you to trust your team mates and fight 'til the very end. Let us lift the school spirit up, and let us win this game. Are you guys ready?

Ready!!

So what are all waiting for? Let us go out there, and let's show them what we are made of.

** ** ** ** ** ** ** ** ** **

So the game has finally began, it's a good thing he's not making me one of the first five. I'm not yet ready; I need to condition myself first. I have to put in mind that I can do it, I'm invincible. I am not alone, they are with me, I am a heart, and I can conquer a—

"Garcia, in the court now, change with Mr. Mendoza"

And I was about to enjoy myself sitting in this bench, and thinking what I should do next.

"Yes sir!"

Well here goes nothing. Remember Cassey you are not alone in this fight. You can do it.

Here she goes. Oh Lord please help her play, make her play like before.

This is her time, to prove herself, I hope that it's not a mistake to listen to that Steve Turner; he's in this big time. I sure hope he knows exactly what he's doing.

This is your time to shine once more, be that heart once more. Play like you never played before.

Who is that lady? Is woman even allowed in men's game?

Well this is it, my time to shine once more. Let's show this people what I'm capable of. Here I go! I know I can do it, with all their help, I won't disappoint them.

Stepping in my stadium with all this players to play with, shook my knees, I began to tremble and not only that I thought of going back to the bench and ask the coach if I could leave, but when I saw Coach Turner, everything changed. I regained my strength, my knees stop trembling, and the most unbelievable thing happened. I'm playing my favorite game at my stadium, with ease in my heart and with confidence boosting me and my team mates. I know we can make it through. I know nothing bad will happen. And I know we can win this game. I've got so much more to give, and so much more to show.

She's really different when she's playing, as if she has her own little world, and nothing exist on it except her and that game. She's one truly amazing woman. If I don't know, I wouldn't believe when they'll tell me she stopped playing because of an injury, it's simply is unbelievable with the way she plays right now.

** ** ** ** ** ** ** ** ** **

I couldn't believe I've made it this long. I never run this much, and play this much since the incident before, not even in practice. Everything seems lighter in practice, at first I thought I was out of shape that I can't play this game anymore. But with each passing time, I regain my posture and I'm all set to go. I played like I never played before, I played to my fullest and I played with all my heart. Sweat, fatigue, body aches, all were nothing compare to the happiness I'm feeling right now. I feel so complete. I feel me again.

With every shot I made, I feel lighter. With every successful assist, my heart feels glad. With every opponent I passed through, I feel complete. I felt like I never did before. So this is how it feels to play real basketball, to play my one and only love. This is how it feels to live yourself again. I feel that I was reborn in this world, I feel so light and so peaceful. There is nothing more than I could ever ask for, but to let this moment stay forever. I hope.

I hope time will freeze, and never let this moment wither; to let this moment stay forever.

** ** ** ** ** ** ** ** ** **

Here goes second half. I hope she could still make it.

Can she still play? She looks tired, I better switch her with the regulars, but Steve's giving me that look. *Sigh* I guess I got no choice; I have to let her play.

I have my confidence with her, but can her body take it? It has been a long time since she played like this, and even better.

Heavy breathing I hope he'll let me sit for a while, I think my body wouldn't make it anymore.

"Could that girl still make it, she looks so tired and way out of shape?"

"She shouldn't have played with them in the first place."

"What is she trying to prove anyway? She's a woman for goodness sake!"

"Leave her alone! Can't you see how good she is? If you aren't going to say something nice, just keep your mouth shut. Geez! You just talk and talk without even looking." Mark exploded.

The murmurs ended.

Aaww He's such a nice guy after-all. He really knows how to make someone feels so special.

Finally that stupid whisperings stopped. It has already been too much pressure for her to play in this game, and they're making it heavier. They just don't know what she's feeling, all they could do is to judge everyone on this court, and I bet they don't even have the slightest idea on what's happening on the court right now.

My body's sore, and I can't catch my breath anymore, it's becoming too difficult for me to play. I think my body is at its limit, I have to rest or else I'm going to fall. My team mates must have noticed it by now, but they keep on letting me handle the ball, I'm too tired.

Oh no! I have to switch her, I don't care what Steve thinks anymore, I'm risking it too much, I'll be at risk if anything happens to her, I'm pushing her too much. She won't make it.

I don't care anymore of what would happen I'm going to drive this ball and then take my bow and exit. This will be my last shot, I have to make it. But—

** ** ** ** ** ** ** ** ** **

This was the same attitude I have before. Never caring about what would happen next. I was too tired and the clock is ticking fast, I can't spare a second to breathe. I took the ball and drive it hard to the other side of the court. Stupid! I know. I was stupid back then, I was so tired and yet I did a coast to coast, I never thought someone would care to follow me, even at my jump. And right there and then I lose everything. No one seems to care at that moment, it's either they're too tired to run beside me, or they just simply didn't care, because the buzzer went off and we had won by a point.

At that very moment I felt so alone; for the first time in my life I felt I was on my own, with no one to look out for me not even in the shadows. At that same moment I felt that I should learn to stand up on my own and never trust anyone except for myself. I hid myself, and lived in the shadows for a long time. I never thought I'd be coming out of my own little world, but some things are just meant to happen. Some things are meant to be learned, to make life more interesting. And this was the truth that is hard to accept.

** ** ** ** ** ** ** ** ** **

Sigh I'm not the same as before, I'm doing this to prove something, and to make my stay worthwhile. I know I can do this; nothing's going to happen; besides I'll make sure I won't do anything stupid this time. I'll drive then make that shot and then leave the court. Wait! That's embarrassing, make it step to the benches and say I can't make it anymore. That sounds a good plan.

What is she trying to do? Is she forcing herself? This is stupid!

"Mr. Cruz, switch with Ms. Garcia."

"Yes coach!"

What is she doing? Is she finally facing her fears? Will she really drive the ball?

"Look at her, trying to be Miss showy!"

Whispers started again, but Mark didn't do anything as he watch intently what she is about to do next.

Well here goes nothing. For my final bow

**   **   **   **   **   **   **   **   **   **

I'm in the perfect mood, perfect pace, I was in the zone and then it snaps! I wasn't able to finish the drive, my body already had enough, my knee took its toll, and I just had to fall. Poof! My final bow had disappeared in front of my very eyes. But I was not alone. Everyone cared to help me up, even our opponents; maybe because I'm a lady and they're just trying to be gentleman. That was the first thing that came into my mind, but then I saw their sincerity. But I didn't want to stand up; I want to feel the cold floor once more, but this time in the warmer side of it. When reality hit me, that I was taking too much time lying there, I decided to urge into standing up. Everyone tries to help me but I spoke the words I never thought I could say.

"I. Can. Still. Make. It." I stared them wide-eyed shock from my own words

83

"Are you sure?"

"Yes, I have to finish the shot, I have to."

"Why?"

"Because I, Cassandra Bernadette Garcia, never back out to a fight, this is my time. This is my moment to redeem myself and to face my future once more. I have to make that shot"

"Is that so? Then let's see if you can pass through me" Number five said.

I smiled and accepted his challenge, I won't back down easily. I'll make that shot whoever goes in my way. For the very first time, I felt like a true player. I never felt this good even before, I never felt this warm and so contented.

Finally, she has stand back up on her feet. I can now sleep peacefully at night.

She's amazing. I can't believe she still wants to continue this shot. Steve was right, there is more beneath what is seen outside. She's outstanding, brilliant!

She finally admitted she's Cassandra, she's back to her normal self now, and finally my work as a number one fan has paid off. She's smiling again.

"Wow! That's one tough girl" Clapping her hand loudly, and slowly standing up

Clapping gets louder. Standing ovation is observant.

They're all clapping *sniff* I'm finally being appreciated. *Sniff*

**   **   **   **   **   **   **   **   **   **

After I made that shot, I was immediately brought to the nearest hospital, the coach was terrified, he said something about bones being broken, or was it tendons. I really don't care about all that at this point of my life. All I cared about right now is that I made that shot, I faced my fears, and finally now, I can see my future as bright as ever before.

Mark called to say that we won, but he didn't tell me the score. Maybe because he didn't want me to know that I was not so much of a help for them. And here I am sitting in the hospital bed, waiting for my parents to come. Bet that the first thing they'll say is "Have you gone mad?" or something like "What got into your head?" Parents! They never let their children know they care, sometimes it make us children feel that we aren't even cared about. I just hope that parents would be showy sometimes.

"Hey, are you alright honey?" A sweet melancholic voice said.

"Excuse me? What did you just said?" Looking at her wide-eyed

"I said are you alright honey, why? What's wrong?" She asks with concern

"You never call me honey."

"Yes I do, I called you honey when you were a little girl, and when you reached high school you told me you're too old to be called honey, that is why I stopped"

"Did I? Why are you not mad at me about this?"

"Why should I?"

"Well because it was stupid of me, and because you got mad at me the first time it happened."

"That is simply because that was stupid of you, and I don't know the details, unlike today I knew everything that had happened"

"Who told you? How"

85

"Mark called me to say that you're being rushed to the hospital, he explained everything to me so no need for me to be that hysterical mother you're talking about."

"And?"

"And—I'm proud of you for standing up, and for doing just that. This is not stupidity, its bravery, and I admire you of that." Smiling brightly to her daughter

"You *sniff* you're proud of me? *Sniff*"

"Yes, very much" Smiling warmly

"Thank *sniff* you"

"Why are you crying?" Hugging her tightly, letting her cry to her shoulder

"You never seem to care, neither do you even tell me you're proud of me nor you appreciate what I'm doing. It's the first time I ever heard those words and it feels so good. Ma, I'm sorry for being so distant this past three years, I'm sorry for—"

"No need to say sorry, I knew exactly how it's been." Smiling at her gently rubbing her back

"Thank you"

Feeling my mother's hug was the best thing I ever felt for the past three years. I'm regretting the moments I wasted on that stupid hiding. But at some point I'm glad that it happened, because if it didn't I don't think I'll ever take that hug with such importance, and it wouldn't feel that way. It was special, the best hug I got since I could remember. I feel so contented. If it wasn't for this bet, I wouldn't be experiencing all this. I wouldn't be able to show myself once more, I wouldn't be able to stand back up and to face my fears, and most importantly I wouldn't feel my mother's hug if it wasn't for that bet.

Oops! Wrong timing, my bad. I better get out of here. She's so lucky to have a mother like her. A mother that always looks out for her, and giving her that kind of hugs. I hope my father was the same, but he died along with my mother. *Sigh* no use in hoping for something so impossible. I just have to accept the fact that I would never have a complete family. Unlike hers

-13:30-

Looks like it's the right time for me to visit her; there's nothing more to disturb. Let me see. *Sigh* still isn't the right time. Her family is inside; I simply can't go in and act like I'm a part of them. Even though I live with them this past few days, it still doesn't give me the right to barge in, it's just isn't right. Might as well forget about it, and comes back later this day, or better yet just text her that I came to visit but—I couldn't possible tell her that. I'll just say that I'm busy, yeah! That's it, I'm busy. *Sigh* that wouldn't work; I have no choice but to come back later.

-15:00-

I hope that she's still here; I would lose my face to her if I didn't get to visit her while she's still here. *Sigh* I'm so hopeless, I'm trying to be hopeful and yet I stare down on the floor that I'm walking on.

"Mark is that you?" A soft voice asks

"Cassey?" Turning his head

"What are you doing here?"

"I came to visit, sorry about being so late, oh by the way for you" Handing her a plastic bag

"I don't think I could hold that, I kind of have my hands full as you can see" Showing off the crutches

"Sorry about that, let me help you."

"Thank you, I can still manage, I used to use this crutches before"

"How long would you be using that?"

87

"Oh this? Just a few days I think, to have my knee relax a bit"

"Oh! That's good, so you'll recover quickly."

"Yes, thank you"

I never thought I'd enjoy a moment with him/her under this circumstance.

"*Cough* Can I walk you home?" Asking shyly, hoping that she'd say yes

"Are you sure? It's out of your way."

"It's okay if you don't want to I'm not—"

"Sure, I would love that"

"Really?" Smiling brightly at her

It's real nice to have someone to walk with, especially during time like this. I'm so lucky to have him beside me. He's such a nice guy.

I hope we could do this more often, I would really like that, spending afternoon walks with her.

The walk was fun, even though it was quiet. It was very peaceful and though we didn't speak that much, I felt his sincere presence beside me, walking me home, a true friend indeed.

Well here we are. *Sigh* I can't imagine I'm missing this house now; it has been six long days now since I last saw this house. I wonder how everything is. How is she handling my life? I wonder if she knew about my father by now, but I hope that she didn't, I hope she just didn't notice his absence; it would be such a bother to her, if she finds out.

"Well, I better get in" Walking in the front door.

The door slowly opened, and Mark saw the shock of his life.

What is he doing here at this time of day? He's supposed to be at work, why is he here? This can't be happening is it? Does he finally realize my absence? No it couldn't be.

"Why are you here? Aren't you supposed to be working?" Asking in such a harsh tone

"I was about to leave; I forgot something earlier this day, I just went home to get it."

"I'd like you to meet Cassey before you leave. Cassey my dad." He introduces them in a bored tone

"I'm glad to finally meet your father" Smiling at him, then to his father

"He's not a father; he's just a dad, an image." He then retreated slowly waving and said "Bye!"

He's nothing but a dad image; he never did once become a father to me. He work and work and work, all day all night. He didn't have any time for me, I was left alone at that huge house with strangers who took their time to look out for me, and spend time with me, when it should've been his job. I hate him so much, that it pained me to see him. I don't want to see him ever again.

"Mark, wait up!" His father runs after him

"What do you want? Leave me alone!" Using that harsh tone again

"I just want to talk with you, could you please stop walking away from me?" Trying hard to catch up

"Talk about what? We have nothing to walk about so JUST LEAVE ME ALONE!" he finally comes to a halt. He turns back and saw his father running faster to take this advantage.

"Mark, please, let me talk."

"You're already too late; we have nothing to talk about."

"Mark, I'm sorry, for treating you like that, it's just that it hurts me to see you."

"Hurt? You don't even have the slightest idea how hurt I was. When mom died you died along with her, leaving me all alone, on my own."

"It's just that you look exactly like your mother. You even sound just like her when you were just a child, and you remind me so much of her. It hurts me to see you because I couldn't accept the fact that she died."

"That was a long time ago, I understood that when I reached the age of twelve, I waited for you to come back but you never did. It's already too late for that now."

"I'm sorry, I'm so used to working all day long I forgot that someone is still waiting for me at home, until finally you got tired of waiting, I'm sorry."

"Sorry is not enough. I hate you!" Slowly tears fall down to his cheeks.

"Is that really what you feel? Can't I do anything anymore?" Feeling defeated

"I hate you; I don't want to see you anymore." Running away from him; running away from the hurt.

Honk! Honk! Honk!

Everything is a blur; what is going on? Why is that man cover in blood; what am I doing here? What happened? How did I end up on the ground aargh! That lady she screams of my--

~Chapter 7: Sunday~

Yawn Where am I? This isn't my room or Cassey's. Aargh! My head! It hurts! What happened? I feel like I pound my head a thousand times. Huh? Why am I covered in bandaged? Aargh! I can't seem to remember anything that had happened except for a forceful push that somehow made me lie down face flat on the ground. And when I was able to open my eyes all I see was a man covered with blood, but I couldn't picture who it was and then all of a sudden I blacked out. The last thing that I heard was a screaming lady.

"*Yawn* I can't believe I've fallen asleep" Stretching her arms and legs as she stands from the bench she had slept in for the night. I hope they're alright. I hope that both of them could go home safe and sound. How I wish that it'll be a minor injuries for the both of them.

Croak w-where am I? What is this place? M-Mark, where is he? I have to—Aargh! My body, it hurts. I-I can't move. (Looking disorientated)

"Don't move so much, you're badly injured. You're lucky to be alive after that hit." A man in white said in concern, while trying to calm him.

"W-what happened?" He asks in confusion.

"You were hit by a truck trying to save your son's life."

"My son? Mark?! Where is he? What happened to him?"

"He's alright, he's on the other side, sleeping I presume."

"Thank God!" sighing in relief.

"I'll be going now, don't try to move as much for now." He ordered.

"Thank you." He says with so much gratitude.

Thank God Mark is alright. I wouldn't forgive myself if he isn't. I hope the doctor was really telling the truth, I wouldn't be able to handle it if it were a lie. I wonder how he is handling himself right now. What are his thoughts? Would he blame me for all this?

Where is my father? Why isn't he here? He should be visiting me; doesn't he care for me anymore? So I was right after all, he wasn't really that serious when he asks for forgiveness, they were all lies. He doesn't care about anyone except for himself and his stupid job! I hate him so much; I wish he wasn't my father.

Oh Lord please save them both, they both have unfinished business with each other, they still need to make up. You would allow it would you? Oh please say yes, I still need him, and they still need him. Many still needs Mr. Rivera, save them please? I wished both of them are okay, now who should I visit first? Should it be the one on my right or the one on my left? This is a difficult one. Hmm... I guess I'll go to the one on my left first.

"Good morning Mr. Rivera" She said softly, while entering the room as quiet as she could.

"Good morning Cassey, nice of you to drop by" Smiling at her with genuine sincerity.

"How are you feeling sir?" She asks filled with concern

"I'm alright, I can live. How is Mark?" He asks anxiously

"I still don't know, I check on you first, do you want me to check up on him now?"

"Yes please, thank you" He smiled.

"I'll be right back" She slowly leaves the room quietly as possible.

Wow! Mark is so lucky to have a father like him that worries so much for him. He could've died right there and then, and now as he wakes up the first thing on his mind is his son's safety. What an incredible father he is. I can't believe parents would go to such extent for their child. Would I also be like that when I become a parent? Why do they do such things? I wonder why. Well here goes, I hope he's awake.

"Mark, are you awake?" Asking in a soft voice while entering the room quietly as possible

"Yeah, I am, why?" He asks a bit irritated.

"Did I wake you up?" Feeling sorry about it

"No-No. It's alright, why are you here?" He smiles warmly

"I came here to visit, and check up on you, so how are you feeling?" She asks brightly

"I'm fine, thank you, I can live." He smiles more.

"That's good to hear." She sighs in relief.

"So, where is my dad?" He asks coldly.

"He's on the other side of this room" She answers honestly.

"Tsk! He took the time to visit someone else over his own son? How dare he?" He said colder

"He's not visiting anyone; he's also a patient here"

"Why? Did he have a heart attack for running so much? Ha! Serves him right!"

"How dare you say that?! You don't know anything do you?" She looks at him sternly.

"What? What's with that look?" He raises a brow.

"He risks his life saving you and this is all that he gets?" She said anger filling her voice.

"That would be something that he wouldn't do, besides I can't quite remember everything that had happened." He looks at her innocently, trying to ask her what happened.

93

"You were almost hit by a truck, you were lucky that your father got there in time."

"Stop saying something stupid would you? All he cares about is him and that stupid job of his, I am nothing to him and that will always be the case." Obviously hurt was heard

"You obviously don't know anything." She shook her head looking at him with disbelief.

"It's you who doesn't know anything." He said trying to avoid her stare.

"Whatever, I'm leaving" She turns to her heels and leave.

"Hey, where are you going?" Trying to reach her, and make her turn back, but it was disregarded.

I can't believe I even regarded him being nice and all that, I was so wrong. He's nothing but a jerk. How dare he say that to his father, who risks so much for him. Tsk! He's so lucky to have a father like that and all he does is whine, how dare he?! If I were in his father's place, I would rather leave him alone and let him die on the spot, who is he anyways? He doesn't even recognize me in the first place. Aargh! He's such a jerk!

What is her problem? She wasn't the one who felt all those pain throughout those years. She got no idea how I handled it and how much it hurts me still up to this day. How would she? She has both her parents who loves her so much and will always remain beside her whatever happens. She would never know because it was not her who suffered, it was me and I know better. Don't tell me I don't know anything, because I do.

-10:00-

"You're alright now and your bruises will heal in no time. You're good to go" The doctor said after he examined him.

"Thanks." He manage to say

"Welcome, oh and your father is on the other side." He said before turning away.

"Why are you telling me this? It's not like I would go visit him or something." He said as a matter of fact

"Excuse me?"

"It's not like I'm going to visit him, what's the use of telling me where he is?"

"He is your father, that's enough reason to visit him right?"

"Yeah, father in papers." He snorted

"I may not know the rift between you and your father, but one thing I know is that he is there right now because of you." He said in an angry voice.

"Yeah right, as if he would really do that." He shook his head.

"You kids nowadays think you know everything, but let me tell you this, you don't. There are a million things you still don't know, and you wouldn't know."

"You don't have the right to tell me that because you don't know anything."

"Maybe I don't, but I do know something, someday when the time is right, you would regret everything. And when that time comes there's no way turning back, so before it even arrives why not try to patch some things with your father. You may not know it but parents are the essential part of their children. A child would never be complete without a parent." He said, and finally leaves him in his thoughts.

Who is he anyway? He's just a doctor, besides not because he cured me means I'm giving him the right to meddle with my affairs, or even to dictate me and lecture me. He's just nobody anyways, someone whom I will never meet again and yet why am I feeling this way? Why did I get hurt with his words? Why do I felt like what he's saying might be true? His words—it pierce deep into my heart, why is that? Am I being guilty? Maybe that's just it, I'm guilty. But guilty about what, I didn't do anything to him, it was his choice anyways not my fault. And yet, why do I feel that it's my fault? Is it?

**   **   **   **   **   **   **   **   **   **

I was so young when I lose my mom, I was depressed because I lose not just my mother, I also lose one of my best friend, and no one told me why. It was later that I found out she died due to her bad health. Everyone told me that everything would be fine, because I still have my father, he would take good care of me and would make me feel like that mom was still alive. As a child I believe on those words, I keep my hopes up but they were all lies, none of them told me the truth. Because not only did I lose my mother, I also lose my father at the same time.

He started to work overtime, that I hardly gets to see him. He would go home when I'm already asleep, and he would go out early in the morning and sometimes when I'm already out to school. Everything changed since then, my family was shattered into tiny little pieces that are impossible to be fixed.

I tried to be a better son, I behave properly and I wait for him to return, especially when I don't have classes the next day. But I was too young; no one could blame me if I drift off to sleep while waiting. And at a young age, I force myself to accept that things will never be the same, that it was my fault that my father wasn't home. I started to neglect his absence, I started to get used to being alone. That at one point I started to hate him.

Yes, at a very young age I hated him already. It was our school day, everyone got their parents with them and there I am sitting all alone in one corner of our classroom waiting for everything to finish. I was the only one there who hasn't brought his parents over for the activity, and I was the only one who got left behind, and got neglected. I hated him for that, because he let me suffer it all alone, he left me by myself and the worst of all I still couldn't forget the embarrassment I went through. Because after that day, everyone at school teases me for not having a parent on school day, it was simply too painful.

And then the rest was history, I can't even remember the things that I hate about him. All that I could remember was the start which is too petty. But through the years it has grown, I had nurtured it, and I blame him for that. I blame him for everything that went wrong. I blame him

96

because I couldn't accept the fact that it was I who's at fault. It was I who neglected him, not the other way around. He never did neglect me, he tried to reach out but I refused to. I was a stone back then, and even at this point, but it still doesn't change the fact that I wanted my apology. The apology I needed way back, I want an apology for the very same reason why I hated him in the first place.

Petty, I know. But I can't help it, deep inside me I just couldn't let it go. I still couldn't accept the fact that I lose my best friend at the very young age. It has distorted the trust that I could've given to those who needed them and those who deserves them. It has destroyed my younger days, because I felt pain throughout childhood because of their teasing. I lost a part of me, when I let it all go.

It have been so many years, maybe it's about time for me to let it all go. This is the time for me to forgive and forget, and finally to reconcile with my father, or at least to hear him out. He deserves it anyways. He deserves it not because he saved me from my near death, but because he is my father. No matter how much I hate him, or how hard I try to turn everything and change everything there is to change, the fact will always remain a fact and that is no matter how hard I tried, he'll always be my father, and no one else could be him.

** ** ** ** ** ** ** ** ** **

Maybe I was being too judgmental; he has every right to say those things anyways. He is after all the one who experienced all those, and he is Mr. Rivera's son. I'm in no right to meddle with stuffs like this. This is way too personal, and I made the wrong move in meddling with it. I should go back and say that I'm sorry. Maybe it's still not too late. Maybe I could help him out, in sorting his feelings.

I should go visit him, since he's just on the other side, but it will be too awkward. Beside I don't have any reasons to visit him. He knew too well how much I hate him; my cover would easily be seen. I need an excuse. I need to have a disguise; I shouldn't let him see my purpose just yet.

-12:00-

I hope he likes this kind of food. Picking out something to let him eat was hard; I grew up not knowing what he likes to eat, or what kind of food he doesn't like. Well, here's my disguise, now my only problem is how to start a conversation with him. We never had any talks, the only talk we had was yesterday, and that's not so healthy. I'm his child, so it's my job to initiate this talk, I just got to or else nothing good will happen, it would just get worse, and I'm already tired of it, I'm tired of being angry at him.

I hope they're both alright, and I also hope that he would still talk with me after everything that I have said and done earlier. Here I go, fruits on my hand and apology ready in my mind. I can do this, for him I have to do it.

Standing out this door made me feel stupid. Why am I all shaky and nervous all of a sudden? I'm just going to talk with my father, nothing to be scared about right? This is really stupid, I shouldn't be feeling this way, and I shouldn't be trembling and acting so weak. I have to let him see that I am strong, that I can stand up on my own, but then where will he fit in as my father? Aren't parents supposed to be their child's strength? Is this okay? That I let him feel that he's needed? Even though I don't know why I am feeling like this? Aargh! Never mind let this get over and done with.

Is that Mark? What is he doing with that paper bag in his hands outside his father's room? Is he finally going to reconcile with him? Or is he going to do something terrible? Oh no! I'm doing it again, meddling with his stuffs. Stop it Cassey, you don't have the right, your only role is to watch and listen, nothing more. No more speaking for you, you've already done so much. Now Cassey, let's leave them both alone, but I'm very curious as to where this will lead. Peeking wouldn't be a crime would it?

** ** ** ** ** ** ** ** ** **

"Hey! How are you doing?" Saying as cheerfully as he can

"H-hey!" Struggling to open his eyes

"Sorry to wake you up, I'll just come back later." Trying to run away

"No it's okay, please stay. I would like some company." He smiled

"Okay, if that's what you want."

Silence filled the room.

"So, I brought you lunch, hope that you like this kind of stuff." Breaking the silence that forms within them

"Thanks, but the doctor told me not to eat anything yet"

"Oh, well then I'll just—" Disappointment filled his voice.

"No leave it, I'd eat it as soon as I can eat, I promise." Trying to bring his spirit up

"If you say so" He put it on the nearby desk

"How are you? How are your injuries?" He asks concern

"I'm fine, my injuries are well taken care of, the doctor released me earlier, there's no need for me to stay here he said." Trying as hard as he could not to look at his stare

"That's good to hear, that's the first good news I heard all day, thank you"

"Huh? Thanks for what?" Looking at him puzzled.

"For the good news, for being safe, and most of all for being here right now" He smiles warmly

"It's no big deal" He look at the walls

"But it is, it's the first time we ever had this conversation, and it's really heartwarming to know that you care." He smiled even brighter

"Yeah, it's the first" Trying to look down.

"We should do this more often, it feels nice." He suggested

"It feels awkward; I'm not used to it sorry." He said looking straight into his father's eyes.

"I know, but at least it's a start."

"Yeah, a start" He continued to stare into his eyes.

The room is filled with silence for a moment, until they both heard a noise outside.

"What are you doing there eavesdropping?" He asks raising a brow

"I- I p-planned to visit you guys but then I heard you talking so-so I kind of listen, sorry" Looking at the floor, shyly answers him.

"Come on in."

"Thanks" Smiling at him warmly.

"I believe you weren't formally introduced, Cassey meet my father, dad I'd like you to meet Cassey." Both of them look at him wide-eyed, shocked with what he had said.

"What? Did I say something wrong?" Looking for answers

"It's just that, you called me your father": He answers in teary eyes.

"Yeah, I know and I'm very sorry that it took me a long time to say it." He says shyly.

"No, don't apologize; I'm just glad that you did." He smiled brightly.

"Thanks, for everything, for saving my life back there and for caring about me right now." He said slowly while trying hard not to let a tear drop fall.

"Of course, you're my son; I won't let anything happen to you." He smiled and asks for a hug

"Thanks dad." He hugs him and finally letting his tears slowly fall down.

I can't believe I'd cry in moments like this. I acted tough, I always show my tough side, but then everything came crashing down before me. I've finally let my soft side shown. I've become as transparent as them, and I'm starting to tear the mask off my face that has been hanging there for a very long time now, and I don't feel ashamed of it. I'm actually glad at the thought of it, finally letting all this emotions out at the same time. I'm finally letting it all go. It felt so good like this, hugging your parent. I hope we could do this again.

It's like watching a movie, and the ending's good. They've finally reconciled. I'm happy for them, there is no more room for me here, might as well leave this fruits at the table and then leave them alone, to enjoy each other's company for a while, 'til it lasts.

"Hey! Cassey thanks." He smiled at him while wiping his tears

"No need to thank me, I didn't do anything." She smiled back

"You did a lot actually, thank you" His father said

"It's nice to know that I could be of any help, well I think I'd be going now. Take care Mr. Rivera." Waving good-bye

"Mark, why don't you walk Cassey home?" Giving him that odd look

"There's no need for that, you need Mark here." She protests

"Can you handle it alone?" He asks concerned

"Yes, I can manage, walk her home already."

"Really, there's no need for that." She protests, but it was fruitless

"Come on Cassey, let go." Inviting her

"Okay, guess that I have no choice anymore." She follows.

**　　**　　**　　**　　**　　**　　**　　**　　**　　**

"Thanks again for everything Cassey" He smiled warmly.

"As I said earlier, there's nothing to thank for, I did nothing" She smiled back

"Just-- thanks!" He breathes out.

"Oh yeah, about the bet" She remembers

"Well, we both switch back even before the last day." He starts to think

"Well, I lose then since I was the first one to fail the conditions." She sighs

"Let's make it a win-win situation since we both failed to complete it." He smiles, cheering her up

"But still, I was the first—

"Doesn't matter, we both failed it, no one loses and no one wins, win-win situation, don't you agree with me" Looking at her intently, waiting for her to say yes.

"If you say so, then okay it's a win-win" She tried to smile weakly.

"We're here; I'd be going back now."

"Be careful okay?" Sounding concern

"Yeah, I' will" He chuckles

"Mark, thank you very much" She whispers as she hugs him tight, which he hugged in return.

It's like walking in dream land, where everything turns out right, where everything just falls in their rightful place; I hope that when I wake up everything still is the same, because I like it more this way.

I hope that when tomorrow comes, it won't change back to the way it used to be. This scene is perfect the way it is. I hope it'll last forever. And if this is just a dream, I hope that I will never have to wake up again.

~Epilogue~

Thirty seconds left on the clock, and they're down by two, what would Cassey do now? Does she still have a trick left up in her sleeves? She's been practicing hard for this, she prepared for this, because this is her last chance, the chance that she had waited for so long. The time for her to finally redeemed her pride and reclaims her shine. She deserves this; she earned it with her year of hard work and perseverance.

This is it, thirty seconds away from victory; I just hope that I wouldn't be caught. This is the last trick I have in store, no more show time for me. This is the last and the finale of my hard work. I have to acclaim my victory. I'm not alone, he's there smiling at me, cheering for me together with his father and my family. I won't let them down. They believe in me too much to even disappoint them.

Everyone went silent, and then the crowd roar at the sound of the buzzer. Game's over, and they won.

She's sly as a fox, I couldn't believe she'll do that, faking it into a drive and then taking a step back for a three point. That was too much of a risk; thank goodness it's a basket. She's really something. *Laughs* She really is something; the whole team was something during the game. They showed everyone that they deserve to win, they deserve to be called champions, and she deserves to be called MVP. I'm so proud of her.

** ** ** ** ** ** ** ** ** **

It has been a year since that bet we made, and still the lessons lived with us through this day. Cassey grew closer to her family, and they begin to appreciate each other more. While I and my father are okay now, we've patched thing up and we became the best of friends like when I was still young; we even challenge each other once in a while to cook something for the other one's pleasure. It's really nice to have that family that I have hoped and prayed for.

Everything went perfect from worst. Everything was like a dream back then but all this is reality now. I'm not saying that there are no more problems that are occurring, there still is, but it's

104

not like before anymore. I'm not alone now, I now have my father beside me and in addition to that I even got a second family and the best of all is I have a true friend that will stay by my side forever. Even though she still believes that I'm a jerk.

Cassey and I became the best of friends after that swap thing. Though I still pull pranks on her, that she still gets mad at me. But this time, it's not a prank just to have a laugh but a prank that shows my friendly affection towards her. And she in return just asks for breakfast every morning, she says she missed the breakfast at home during the swap, she even said that, that toast was the best she had ever tasted in her life.*Laugh* She's so childish.

** ** ** ** ** ** ** ** ** **

Yawn I'm so tired, I want to sleep. The game's too stressful, it's too tiring but it was worth it. We won, I am named MVP and I did my very best in this game, that's all that it matters anyways. But then the most important thing is that they're all here, I never felt this way before but I believe that they are the reason why I played my hardest this day. They are the reasons for everything I have worked hard for. He was the source of my strength, he always lift my spirit up when I'm down. He never falters in believing in me.

He remained at my side even at the darkest moment in my life. He was very patient with me, and he helped me a lot. He had given up so much for this chance. He gave up his name, and popularity in befriending me, and he gave up some of the time he could've spend with his friends in helping me at practice. He was like my personal coach who looks out for me and pushes me to the extent of my limit. He is the reason why I persevere, because I didn't want to disappoint him, I didn't want to put all his efforts to waste. And besides, he's been nice to me, bringing me breakfast every morning, which somehow made me think that this is his payment for all those pranks he's been pulling off every now and then. *Laughs* such childishness of his.

** ** ** ** ** ** ** ** ** **

It has been a year already but I feel like it was just yesterday when we made that bet. It's funny when I think about it. We were stupid and childish at that point of our lives, but after that week's swap we became mature, and we understood more than we could've understood in our lives. I learned to live once more, and to fight once more. It was a wonderful experience that I would bring the lessons with me 'til the day I die. I would never forget that, because it helped me mold myself to the person I am today. It was truly an eye-opener, and a shocking reality that made me realize things I never knew of.

I saw thing which I ignored before. It has taught me how to trust again, and how to trust myself. I learned to forgive and forget, it had opened my heart, and it had relieved me from the pain and hurt that had been kept inside my heart. I began to feel light and free. I've become the person I wanted to be, not someone whom they want to see. I've become true, not just to myself but to everyone that surrounds me. I've finally shed off my mask.

"Hey! Sorry I took so long" She smiled brightly.

"It's okay; I'm used to it by now, congratulations by the way." He smiled at her brightly.

"What? Congratulations only? I was expecting something more." She playfully pouted

"*Laugh* so what do you want?" He laughingly asks.

"I'm kind of hungry and I would really like an ice cream for dessert, would you buy us both desserts?" She asks, staring at him with big puppy dog eyes.

"Sure, I'll buy desserts as long as you buy us lunch, deal?"

"Why do I get to pay much more than you?" Punching him playfully

"You were named MVP, the least you could do is treat me lunch for putting up with you." He said as a matter of fact, while laughing inside.

"Fine, I'll treat you, little coachie." She teases him.

"*Laugh* I'm just playing with you, I'll be the one to treat you, for doing great, you'd treat me dessert later okay?" He suggests, which she quickly agrees upon.

Wow! It really has been a year already, it seems just like it was just yesterday. The saying was true, the more you enjoy life the faster it seems to pass. I couldn't believe so many things have changed since that one week swap. I didn't even think we'll be this close, being close with him didn't even occurred in my mind, I thought it was too impossible.

After that swap, I began to see things in a different light, I learned to open up bit by bit, and I shed off my mask bit by bit until every bit of it was gone. I began to let people come into my life, and explore the worlds of others. I began to have friends; I began to share my life. It was the best experience that I could share to anyone.

"Hey Mark, do you think all this would happen if we didn't made that bet?" She asks out of the blue.

I wonder what his thoughts about all this, a year has passed and we never did talk about it.

"I don't think so; I believed that everything had happened because we made that bet, how about you?" He stares at her waiting for answers.

I wonder what she's thinking. Could it be that she's regretting it?

"*Smiles* I think so too, it was a nice thing that we made that bet."

Truly that bet is a marvel; it helped me realize things I didn't think I would realize if it wasn't for that bet.

"*Smiles* do you think we could still be this close if it wasn't for that bet? What do you think?"

I believe that we became what we are right now because of that bet. Truly everything is predestined; all the choices we make in our lives it will always have an effect that surely will affect our lives in the future.

"I don't think we'd be this close, since we began to be this close after that bet, didn't we?"

107

It's true we only regarded each other as friends after that week.

The last day was the touchiest part of all the week.

** ** ** ** ** ** ** ** ** **

"Here she comes, everyone on position" Her mother asks excitedly.

"I'm home" She shouts not bothering to look what's in front of her.

"SURPRISE" They yelled in unison, which made her stare wide-eyed at them.

"W-what's all this" She asks confused.

"Welcome home honey." Her mother said while she hugged her

"Welcome back Cass, we've missed you" Her father greeted her.

"Don't you have something to say" She said eyeing her brother.

Smiles Hugging her and softly whispers "Welcome back, I missed you"

"*Aaww* you guys, you didn't have to go in such extent." She said teary eyed.

At that very moment I felt that I was really a part of this family, that I belonged here. Even though at some point in my life I've drift away from them, they never seem to turn their back on me, and they remained a family that I could go back into. I finally got the change to go to a place called home.

** ** ** ** ** ** ** ** ** **

We both successfully reached our goals, after that bet, we did it together hand in hand. We practically became like brother and sister, we became inseparable. We made that special bond that

108

no one can really understand except from the both of us, though sometimes it felt like I too don't understand the extent of that bond.

"So how's your dad's therapy going on?" She asks looking at him in the eye

"Fine, actually great, he's doing really great. He has improved a lot; the doctors told us that if these improvements continue he could walk soon." He smiled brightly

"Wow! That's good news, don't worry I'll continue praying about it." She smiled warmly back at him.

** ** ** ** ** ** ** ** ** **

Dad is truly doing great, ever since that day. The last day of our bet was the toughest part of that whole week. How I wished that I could turn backs the time and prevents myself from running away, and then maybe that didn't happen. But then in the end, no matter how much I regret about it, I can't help but be thankful about it, because it made us a way to reconcile and to finally talk heart to heart. Because of the accident, my heart of stone began to melt.

When I came back from the hospital, I bump into the doctor that examined my dad, and he told me that my father could no longer walk because the hit made a severe damage to the nerve ending in his legs and that trauma build up on him. His mind is preventing him from walking.

"What then could we do?" I ask panicky

"We could let him undergo therapy, but it still is not sure." Answering me honestly

"Is that the only choice we got?" I ask again, disappointment filling my tone.

"I'm afraid so."

His words kept vibrating back and forth in my mind, that somehow, I spilled it out to my father. I can't believe that my father would take things lightly; I thought that he would go hysterical about it but he did the exact opposite of it, he took it as calmly as he can.

109

"I'm sorry for all this, if I hadn't--" I said sadness in my tone

"Don't say it; it's not your fault. Besides something good came out of it right?" He tried to cheer me up

"How can you say that? It nearly killed you" My voice became harsh

"I'm not am I? Besides we couldn't do anything about it anymore, it had happened we might as well look at the cup half full. Stop being pessimistic Mark, nothing will come out good with that kind of thinking." He said calmly.

And since then he'd been attending his therapy session. For the past year, just recently he made an improvement, and he continues in doing so. I sure hope that he could be back to normal in no time. And when he did, I hope we could still have that moment as father and son.

**   **   **   **   **   **   **   **   **   **

"Hey Cassey" He suddenly called out.

"Huh?" She turn back to see.

He hugged her tight, leaving her shock for a moment and slowly she smiles and hugged him back.

"Thank you" He whispered softly.

For that moment I felt that the world had stop turning, and when he softly whispered it, I felt that my world began to stop slowly. For that moment only I felt so appreciated, I felt so complete. I have finally acquired the peace I have longed for. At that point all I could think of is...

For that instance only, I never searched for anything more. It made me whole and worth it. For that moment only everything fell perfectly to their rightful place. At that point all I could think of is...

I'm grateful. That one week had made me whole. One week was all that it takes for me to open my eyes and reveal to me what am I to others is not what matters most, but who I am as a person is. What matters most is how I lived my life, not to please others but to be the best that I can be in my own way.

~THE END~

FSC
www.fsc.org
MIX
Papier | Fördert
gute Waldnutzung
FSC® C083411

Zeitfracht Medien GmbH
Ferdinand-Jühlke-Straße 7
99095 Erfurt, Deutschland
produktsicherheit@kolibri360.de

Druck:
CPI Druckdienstleistungen GmbH
im Auftrag der
Zeitfracht Medien GmbH
Ein Unternehmen der Zeitfracht - Gruppe
Ferdinand-Jühlke-Str. 7
99095 Erfurt